THE 12 DAYS OF CHRISTMAS

ALSO BY LINDA JORDAN

Titanian Fury

Falling Into Flight

Love & the Aliens

Aboard the Universe

To the Stars & Back Again

Paradiso Stories

Rescue Mission: Islands of Seattle, Book 2

Come on over to Linda's website and join the fun!

LindaJordan.net

Don't miss a release!

Sign up for Linda's Serendipitous Newsletter while you're there.

THE 12 DAYS OF CHRISTMAS

AN OFF-WORLDERS GUIDE

LINDA JORDAN

METAMORPHOSIS PRESS

For Michael & Zoe

A PARTRIDGE IN A PEAR TREE

Niida sat on her four back limbs on the cool wood
floor of a room called the Community Center. The room was
in the complex where Vert lived and he was hosting the study
group.

The room looked bare to Niida. Walls and floor a bland
green color compared to the vibrant juicy colors of her
home-world, Cassion. So much of Earth lacked color. She
was growing used to it.

Large windows looked out over gardens which consisted
of tall reeds where a large concentration of birds grazed. Vert
had called them Canadian geese. Occasionally the old
human caretaker ran through the tall plants, probably for
exercise, with his dog. The black and white dog chased the
geese who flew a short distance then stopped to fertilize the
plants. The caretaker slowly chased after them. It had
happened again and again since she'd arrived. How much
exercise did an old human need? Or was it some sort of
game? Humans were still a mystery to her.

Niida had arrived early for the meeting. She'd wanted to

make sure to find a large enough space. A year on Earth had taught her that human buildings rarely took her size into consideration. Even though this complex had been built for Unity employees from across the Multiverse, many of them were miniscule. Cassions were not.

The room smelled of Gassian sweat. The cloying flowery smell was given off when they were too hot or under stress. Anything above forty degrees Fahrenheit was too hot for them.

This Gassian just soldiered on. She obviously wanted to learn about humans. and had arrived early as well. Perhaps she had also been concerned about finding a large enough space. Gassians were also large, just a bit smaller than Cassions, although from a completely different section of the multiverse.

Niida wasn't so sure she wanted to learn more about humans. She only had three more months left on this planet and then would go home. Cassion was a mixed blessing. She longed to return to the darkness of the lush forests of Cassion, even though the family would be there to greet her.

Family always created problems for those involved in service to the Unity. They didn't understand that the Multiverse was a massively diverse place. And that coming into contact with so many other ideas had changed her.

She was considering staying for another term in the Cassion Embassy here on Earth just to avoid them. If so, she would need to work harder at understanding humans to help forge those pesky trade agreements.

The others trickled into the room. Off-worlders who'd signed up for this human study group. The only thing all of them seemed to have in common was that they were part of the Unity.

The last one to arrive was the human. She wore the universal green ribbon which meant that for right now, she was female. The ribbon was tied around a single braid on her hair that hung just past an ear. The rest of her hair was cut very short and dyed a lovely shade of turquoise-purple. Humans had no word for that color, but Cassions did. The sound just couldn't be replicated by any human that Niida had found.

The woman was tall for a human and skinny. It looked like she hadn't grown into those bones. She tripped over a chair leg and dropped her pile of belongings. The Catalpan, who wore an orange clip holding his white hair, leapt up to help her.

Catalpans changed gender at will. The next meeting he might be female and wearing a green ribbon instead of the orange clip or pin.

The system was two-fold. Green for female, Orange for male, blue for none of your business. Females wore the color on ribbons, males on clips or pins for those beings who were color blind. The blue color was worn with a chain. The system had been created for Earth. Humans seemed to have a peculiar need to know. Their common language, English, didn't function well without the knowledge.

The Catalpan's four arms had picked up all the human's belonging before she could even catch her balance.

"Oh, thanks," she said.

No one else spoke. The Tantoans were probably annoyed that the human was three minutes late. A grave insult to them.

Being polite to everyone in the multiverse meant having all eight legs attached to something solid. It was a balancing act that Niida had gotten fairly good at. However new entities whose quirks Niida didn't know were continually showing up as new Unity members. She studied hard to keep up.

"Hello everyone," said the human, having recovered her stability. "I'm Lula Pinnock. I'm one of the Earth Languages Translators at Unity. We'll be meeting every Tuesday and Thursday at 19:00. Thursday is two evenings from tonight. Vert has asked me to lead this group and help you learn more about my planet's cultures."

The human glanced at Vert, the Camassan. He dipped his central frond at her. Niida looked away. All Camassans looked like ferns to her. She ate ferns, so had done her best to avoid Camassans, however nice they might be.

Niida watched Lula balance on her two legs. How had humans even survived with only two legs? Niida would have called it a design flaw.

"First, I think we should go around the room and introduce ourselves and talk about why we're each here and also something interesting about those from our home worlds. My interesting thing about humans is that it's for us you are all wearing signals that speak to your gender. Our language hasn't yet evolved completely to include those who are more than one gender or those who change gender. We are grateful for your effort to help us understand and be clear about things. We'll begin on my right with Vert and then go in a circle around the room."

Niida gave a sigh of relief. She'd be last. That would give her time to think of something to say.

"I'm Vert, from Camassa. I'm new here on Earth and thought this would be a perfect way to get to know everyone. This is the first time I've been away from home and I wanted this study group, thinking it would be a wonderful way to learn more about the multiverse and those who live there. I work for the Earth-Camassa Liaison Department at the Camassan Embassy," he said. Then turned to the group of Meazza on his right.

"I'm the speaker for the Meazza. I'm Glitter," he said in a high-pitched squeaky voice. Then named the other four Meazza, who were only as tall as the chair upon which they sat. They all had black beetle-like bodies with hot-pink wings and looked identical except for their gender ribbons and clips or pins. Glitter named the other four Meazza who were: Blueberry, Tinkerbell, Mush and Shoe.

"We love Earth and have been here for six hundred and forty-three name changes. We change our names nearly every human day. Although we understand that can be troublesome for others. We will keep these same names for this group. Among ourselves, we might keep changing names. We all work in the Meazza-Earth Interface Office," he said.

On their right was a Sartalan. A three-meter tall humanoid with bright-white skin on his face, a ruff of fur around the neck and large black eyes. The body was striped white and black and he had a long tail. The Sartalan exuded a strong smell that resembled human peanut butter. Niida could smell it clear across the room.

"I am Magwab. I work security in the Sartalan-Earth Embassy. Which requires delicacy as humans are easily injured. On Sartala we wage war against each other for sport and the losers are part of the victory feast," he said, sitting more erect.

"What part of the victory feast?" asked Glitter.

"The main course," said Magwab. He turned to his right.

The Meazza edged to the side of the chair farther away when Magwab looked the other direction.

"I'm Squip, from Setagea. We love to have fun and try

new things. I'm thrilled to be here and learn about Earthlings. I get to assist in the Setagean Outreach Program, teaching Earthlings about Setagea. My family and I are looking forward to seeing what I learn here. The podlings will be waiting up when I get home to hear all about it. It's even more fun that I get to learn about all of you too," she said, nearly bouncing out of the plastic slime-absorbent chair.

The Setagean was green and round with a bulbous head. She had feelers on top of her head and waved her arms and legs as she spoke.

"Oh, and our podlings have numbers for names. They choose a real name when they reach maturity."

On Squip's right sat a Tolpian. They were reptilian beings. He was dressed in gauzy silver fabric, anchored by blue rhinestone pins which went perfectly with his blue and purple intricately patterned scales. The orange pin looked completely out of place. His face reminded Niida of a chameleon with its blunt snout. He had two arms, legs and a long tail that was wrapped around the back of the chair.

"I'm Asoona," he said. "I am from Tolpia and am honored to be here. I work in the section of our embassy that helps solve problems. We Tolpians come in three genders which we choose as young ones: female, male and neuter. Each relationship we choose to participate in contains one of each gender. Our lives revolve around finding new ways to express our love for ourselves, each other and the world."

Niida had been friends with another Tolpian from the Embassy, who'd moved on to a different planetary post. One of the nicest beings she'd ever met.

Asoona bowed, acknowledging he was finished speaking and turned to the Catalpan.

The Catalpan stood in one fluid motion to speak. He was

a humanoid, just over two meters tall. Lean and lanky, with four arms, two at the base of the neck, two where a human's hips would have been, except that Catalpan's had no joints. It was as if their entire body was flexible and could bend in any direction. The skin was salmon colored, but Niida knew they changed it at will, as they did genders. Silky-white hair sprouted from odd places and was decorated with silver charms and beads which dangled and chimed. Plus an orange hair clip.

"I am Daisy. I work for Unity as an interpreter, as I speak 4,690 different language groups fluently. I'm currently learning Lushootseed Salish, Siksika and Dine. They are from some of the aboriginal tribal peoples of this continent. I want to learn more about Earth's current inhabitants, so I'm here. We Catalpans have a complex gender system ranging from male and female and androgynes and neuters. We shift our genders depending on what suits our lives at the time. Within our culture, this is signaled by our hair. Decorated hair means the Catalpan is presenting as male. Females don't decorate their hair, but have piercings and wear jewelry. Androgynes completely remove their hair. Neuters, who are a large part of our population dye their hair using plants and minerals."

Daisy returned to his chair as fluidly as he'd stood. Catalpans were known for their great facility for languages. They too, used names derived from Earth to make it easy for others to pronounce.

Next came a Duveilian. There weren't many of them on Earth, but Niida had encountered them on other planets. Humanoids with two heads that silently shared thoughts and feelings, they were heavily muscled and had a tentacle on each hip. Even though Niida was across the room, she caught the faint scent of chocolate they all exuded. Chocolate, one of the best things Earth exported. It was farmed on Duveilia as well, but with less success.

"I'm Renata and my other half is Jolie," said the head with long thick creamy-white hair. "We work at our embassy in legal. We write the contracts for our corps who manufacture chocolate here on Earth. We're here to learn more about humans. We love this planet. It's not nearly as crowded as Duveilia. An interesting thing about us, hmmm. Perhaps it's that once we choose a partner, it's for life."

The second head, with short dark hair nodded and turned to the right.

"I'm Kleep. A Tantoan. New on Earth, just arrived last week. I, along with our AI, give presentations to humans about Tantoans. I don't understand Earth's customs at all. So here I am. I am one being, although you see three. One controls sight, another sound, another movement. I contain all three genders. We are always together. If one of us dies, so do the others, as we are so intimately connected. Tantoans see lateness as the ultimate insult. I must adjust. Humans are always late."

The Tantoan looked like vids of stick insects that Niida had seen when first arriving on Earth. The three bodies were about a meter tall and shared a chair.

"I'm Schooos and from Ossia. I wear this suit to protect both the human environment surrounding me and all of you."

The round suit was made of a black material with a clear helmet-like thing over what might be called a head. The Ossian seemed to be made of flames.

"I am a public relations officer for our embassy. Ossians can lower our flames at will. Also we have no gender. We are not offended if you refer to us as it. We do not consider the word an insult."

Niida's head was spinning. She'd never remember all these names or worlds.

"I'm Martha," said the Gassian.

She was three-legged and almost as large as Niida, with a long tail that draped over the chair and lay on the floor behind her. Martha's wooly fur was purple. Which Niida knew meant she was embarrassed, and young. Older Gassians had more control over their emotions.

"I'm from Gassia and at at the embassy to learn how to communicate with humans. I think the most interesting thing about us is our family structure. We have multiple fathers and mothers and a very long adolescence compared to other beings in the multiverse." Martha turned to her right.

"Pyranz is the name. From Ruplovia. Also with legal at the Ruplovian Embassy. Here to understand humans. Ruplovians do not eat plants or use them and are offended by those who do."

Niida felt immediately uncomfortable. She was an herbivore, like all Cassions. She couldn't talk about that then.

Ruplovians had six tube feet like sea stars and a long wide green tube for their body which opened at the top. Inside was a sticky sap-like nectar which attracted insects. Which the Ruplovians then digested. Niida had met one before. This one identified as male, from the orange pin attached to an orange banner wrapped around the tube body. She didn't even want to think about how they had sex.

She realized everyone was looking at her. It was her turn.

"Oh hello. I'm Niida. From Cassion. I work as a negotiator for trade agreements at the Embassy. I've been on Earth a year and still don't understand humans. So, I thought this study group might be enlightening. I can't think of a single thing that's interesting about Cassions. Except maybe our four eyes can move independently of each other. Which comes in handy back home in the forests of Cassion."

"Good," said Lula. "Well, there are a lot of us here. I don't know about you, but that's a lot of information to remember. Humans learn by repetition."

There were some mumbles of assent around the room.

Pyranz said, "Got it all. No repetition needed here."

"Well, I thought we'd begin this group with handing out assignments. In a couple of months, nearly half of the planet celebrates what humans call Christmas, even though few celebrate it as a religious holiday. Also many people either celebrate the Winter Solstice for the northern hemisphere of Earth or Summer Solstice for the southern half. There are also New Year's celebrations close to the same time of year. There's a lot of celebrating happening."

Niida watched Lula looked around. Perhaps to see if they were all paying attention. Daisy had fallen asleep, draped backwards over his chair and was snoring.

"I thought it would be fun if we delved deep into one of the traditions of Christmas, since it's just over six weeks away. People used to sing what were called Christmas Carols to each other. One was called *The Twelve Days of Christmas*. Each day a number of gifts were sent to a true love. I have just now sent you a copy of the words of the song. I'm going to assign you each a lyric to research and you will report back to the group what you think it means."

Niida received the message, but the words made little sense to her.

Lulu stood and walked in front of Niida and said, "You're going to research day number one. And will present your findings at the next meeting."

Then in front of Pyranz. "Day number two. Due two meetings from now."

Lulu went around the entire room and gave people numbers for their days.

"I don't understand the words," said Niida. "I've never heard of a partridge. And why would someone give a person a pear tree? There isn't room in most apartments for trees."

Pyranz said, "No keeping trees in apartments. Cruel."

He glared with small black eyes that pierced her boundaries. Niida didn't like him, but she politely covered it up.

"You will need to research what the lyrics for your day mean. And report at the next meeting. Well, we're out of time. See you Thursday," said Lula.

And she was gone. Took her belongings and fled the room.

Niida looked around. Some of the group began to leave. Others looked as stunned as Niida felt.

What was she going to do? Only three days to figure out what to say. She couldn't do it.

As she took the autovan back to Mrish's Elegant Living Spaces for Larger Beings, Niida went over the song lyrics, trying to understand the meaning.

Why would someone give their *true love* a tree for Christmas? In her time on Earth, Niida had come to understand a little about Christmas. It was based on an ancient religious holiday and colonialism. The conquerers had imposed their religion on pagan lands and their holidays and rituals had consumed the pagan celebrations, even occurring on the same dates. In the case of Northern Europe, Christmas had swallowed up yule and the winter solstice. The pagan symbolism of evergreen trees and holly and ivy had come to epitomize Christmas as it shifted to a secular and commercial frenzy of gift-giving and feasting. That was during the period of rampant excess.

Today the holiday had been diluted by the influx of Unity residents. And the other religions which existed on Earth. As far as Niida knew, the holiday was now celebrated by getting together with family and giving modest gifts, the making of which didn't harm the planet. And eating a healthy meal together. Humans seemed to be more focused on their connections than on material goods. No matter the advertising of elaborate gifts. Most humans weren't that wealthy.

Niida did some research about partridges once she got back to her room. Partridges were ground birds, not tree birds. They were also associated with Athena, a Greek Goddess. Which meant that the symbolism of wisdom and fertility had become embedded in the culture overtaken by Christianity.

The pear tree, she found, symbolized prosperity, health and happiness. And possibly abundance and longevity. Basically, the lover was wishing the woman he courted fertility, health and happiness. Gifts that would ultimately benefit him if he gained possession of her through marriage, as was the human custom in that time period. The males owned the females.

Niida shuddered at the thought. Most humans had just risen out of their barbaric customs. Some of them still lived with them. Still the Unity had opened for them, as they did sometimes for backwards planets which had abundant natural resources.

In this case, Earth had cacao trees, which were very picky about where they grew. Throughout the multiverse, demand outstripped supply.

Earth also had an abundant supply of mollusks. Not only were mussels a delicacy throughout the Unity, but also snails and slugs.

Cassions were herbivores, so mollusks didn't appeal to her, but chocolate was delicious.

Niida thought long and hard about how to present her part of the song at the next study group. There was little she could do that wouldn't insult someone.

She considered leaving the group. A cowardly move, but effective.

On Tuesday after her work at the embassy, Niida walked through one of the human shopping centers. Many humans still enjoyed the experience of searching for gifts in stores. As did many other Unity members.

The place was packed. Niida had a difficult time moving through the crowds. The mass of humans, the constant music, the smells of cinnamon and fir trees overwhelmed her. Everywhere her four eyes looked, she saw images of trees and birds. Snow and candy canes. One store had a funnel-shaped basket of fruit and vegetables, which made Niida's mouth water.

Then an idea came to her. It wasn't a prime 1 idea, but it was the best one she'd had.

It took six shopping trips over the next two evenings, but finally she found all the supplies for her presentation. Niida drew an elaborate sign with the lyrics. Maybe sign wasn't the best description. It was also a chart with all the possible symbolic meanings she'd found for partridge and pear tree.

On Thursday, Niida's supervisor called her to confer.

"You seem distracted yesterday. Is everything fine with you?"

Niida explained about the study group.

"Yes, doing presentations is always so difficult for us. I am pleased you took this challenge upon yourself. Does this mean you'll be staying here for another term?"

"I don't yet know. I am considering it. Family, you know."

"Yes, I do. My family want me home. They believe I am a failure."

"We both know you are not," said Niida.

"Yes. I shall not return to Cassion. Much do I miss the jungles of my homeland. I strive to recreate them in my home here."

Niida nodded. She smiled as the thought of Pyranz's reaction if he could see her room. It was filled with plants in pots of dirt. Many of them reached the tall ceiling with its many skylights. Her room was a humid blooming and tangled jungle. Many of the plants she dined on daily. A small hive of bees lived in one corner, pollinating the fruit, which she also ate. A pear tree wouldn't be out of place.

It took all her four arms to carry the supplies to the meeting room. She was excited to give her presentation and just hoped everyone would be receptive to new ideas. That's why they were at the study group. To learn about humans and their ideas, after all.

She was the first to arrive. So Niida set up her display in the front of the room. Then arranged the chairs in a fan shape around the back and sides, as humans often did. Vert arrived next, since he lived in the complex.

Niida sat on the floor near the display, crossing her four legs and four arms in the meditative posture of Gdep. She closed her eyes and sat, breathing deeply and calming herself. She smelled when Martha entered the room, although the gardenia scent was milder today than it had been on Tuesday.

Niida heard the high squeaky voices of Glitter, Blueberry, Shoe and the other two whose names she'd forgotten, as they fought over who would sit where on their chair.

She could also smell the ripe pears in the silver-colored bowl beside her. It had taken five stores before ripe ones could be found. The pears were imported from another region on Earth because all the ones grown nearby had ripened two months ago. The sweet fruity scent made her mouth water. She'd bought extra and eaten one in the autovan on her way to the meeting.

Niida could feel when Pyranz entered. The room chilled a bit and she could tell he glared at her. Or the bowl of pears. It didn't matter. She was merely presenting what humans did.

And Ruplovians ate meat that was just like her, except smaller. They would all need to practice the tolerance the Unity represented.

Many worlds—many needs.

"Good evening everyone," said Lula Pinnock. "I can see that Niida is ready to tell us about the *First Day of Christmas*. But first I'd like to say a little something about the history of the song and the holiday. You can stay where your are Niida."

Niida nodded.

"The first day of Christmas is December 25 and the last day is January 6, which is also called Epiphany and is another religious holiday for Christians. But Christmas is a much older holiday for Pagans, Wiccans, Druids and the ancient people of Europe, where it began. It was also called Yule and was a celebration of the return of the sun after the shortest day of the year, the Winter Solstice. It's a holiday about rebirth. Now the song is from the 1700's. Hundreds of years after the Pagans were dominant in Northern Europe. The Christians had come into power and the song was probably a memory game, possibly for children. That's the history that we have about it. As Niida does her presentation, I implore all of you to remember the Unity's purpose. We are here to study humans. My ways may not always your ways. *Many worlds—many needs.*"

"*Many worlds—many needs,*" everyone repeated in unison.

"Niida, you may begin," said Lula, sitting on one of the chairs.

Niida stayed sitting, not wanting to intimidate the smaller members of the group. Sitting, she was at eye level with nearly everyone.

"I've gathered representations of the first day. *On the first day of Christmas my true love gave to me a partridge in a pear tree.* Here is a printed partridge that I'll pass around. Humans used to hunt and eat them for their evening meals. The gift of a partridge was the gift of a meal that might feed a small family. Many humans didn't have enough food, so for them it symbolized wealth."

Niida handed the fabricated partridge, round and plump, to Magwab on her right. A replica complete with feathers and glossy eyes. Magwab sniffed it and turned the plastic bird upside down, but his gestures still looked as if he wanted to eat it, before passing it on.

"In the lyric for the first day, the partridge was sitting in a pear tree. I couldn't find a pear tree, but I did find some pears. They are from the southern part of this planet. Humans would eat them both raw and cooked. The gift of a pear tree was food for that season and many more beyond. Perhaps even for a lifetime, as pear trees give fruit year after year. Again, humans didn't always provide for each other, so giving food was very symbolic. Pears are shaped like the heart symbol humans used and partridges were thought to be an aphrodisiac. The song is told from the point of view of the intended, who would have been female, about the gifts she received from a male suitor. He was trying very hard to impress her. I will pass the pears around. If you'd like to take one, please do so. In the very center of the fruit is a core with the seeds. I do not know if they will grow a tree. Humans have done strange things with breeding plants. But at the time of this song, seeds planted in the earth would have resulted in another tree. So fertility is another symbol of this lyric. Does anyone have any questions?" Niida asked as she passed the bowl to Magwab.

Magwab sniffed deeply at the bowl of pears. Then wrinkled his nose and passed the bowl to Squip.

"Deeply offended by this song," said Pyranz, standing. "People eating plants and the fruit of plants is obscene. Why was this song chosen?"

Lula stood and said, "Because we are studying humans. We humans are sometimes a barbaric people, even now. In the past, my ancestors and other humans have done unspeakable things. However none of us come from a planet that is without a dark past if they were judged by some Unity members. No one being can please everyone. *Many worlds— many needs.*"

Pryanz sniffed and said, "Well, I do not like it. Registering my complaint with you."

"I understand," said Lula. "Perhaps the other lyrics will suit you better."

Niida watched as Lula stared at him until he sat down. Then Lula sat too.

"I think that little bird would have been very cute. Do they still exist?" asked Asoona.

"I don't know," said Niida. "The references I used didn't say they were extinct."

"The pear smells so sweet and almost perfumed," said Squip, who was holding a pear, which was now covered with slime.

Niida nodded in agreement.

Finally, her presentation was ended and everyone left quickly. Probably eager to work on their own presentations. She felt relieved hers was over. Now she could sit back and enjoy the others.

There were two pears left in the bowl. She'd brought pears for everyone, but hadn't expected the two carnivores to take one. She packed everything up in a large bag and left the pears on top.

Lula said, "That was an excellent presentation, Niida. I gave you the first day, because I thought you could put something together quickly. And you did, thank you."

Niida nodded and went out to the autovan.

She opened the bag as the vehicle drove her back to Mrish's Elegant Living Spaces for Larger Beings. Taking out a pear, she sniffed the perfume of the fruit. Her stomach rumbled. She ate the fruit, leaving the core intact.

She'd try growing a pear tree from the seeds at home. If it worked, she'd put the partridge in the branches. Her very first Christmas gift.

Home.

Niida liked the sound of that. She'd be staying here.

Indefinitely.

TWO TURTLE DOVES

Pyranz wasn't making enough sap. A fly rumbled around in his second chamber. The digestive juices either weren't strong or deep enough to drown and digest his prey. At least it couldn't get out.

"This study group is stupid. All the others are ignorant. I must come up with a presentation to show them how brilliant I am."

He returned to the screen in his apartment, digging his six tube-like feet deeper in the rocky soil to anchor himself. If he could afford a better apartment, the soil would be better. Right now he was a lowly clerk in legal and at the bottom of Level 7. Working his way up to the top of Level 7.

At his last review, Pyranz had been told he didn't have a sufficient understanding of humans to move up. So he'd signed up for this pathetic study group. What did an ancient holiday song have to do with overseeing human contracts here and now?

His time would be better spent taking another law course. However, his superiors would be impressed with him acting on their observations. So here he was trying to sort out a foolish song lyric.

Turtle doves symbolized love. Pyranz didn't understand love. It was a human concept. Ruplovians didn't feel emotions. They felt sensations caused by lack of food, moisture or light. Those were caused by the environment and were real. Emotions seemed to come from within, from what Pyranz had been able to find out.

In later centuries, the text said, the connection with love came partly because dove rhymed with love. English was a peculiar language. Ruplovian was clear and concise with its meanings. English was a mixture of many language groups and had been twisted and turned to suit those in power. In addition too much of it was symbolic, a concept Pyranz was only just coming to understand.

He stretched and the fly finally became so sloshed with digestive juices that it drowned. A relief, even if his juices were weak.

After hours of research, Pyranz gave up and decided to rest. It was going to be a long day tomorrow. He'd need to create the presentation. After working all day.

The next day, Pyranz woke early as usual. He ambled through the park, searching for wild insects, but had no success. The weather had grown too cold for them. This was not the tropics where food was available outside year round.

Back on Ruplovia, those living in colder areas had bodies that went dormant during the cold times, which were rare. Their minds continued on. Thinking deeply and discovering the great truths that existed in the Multiverse. Pyranz had longed to be chosen as a deep thinker. His application had been declined.

His mind *was* keen enough for researching contracts and

other legal matters. He was deemed not to have a mind that was best for finding or constructing the new, but in delving into the past.

He could not change that rating.

Outside the Ruplovian Embassy, he passed through layers of security. They checked for damaging liquids and solids first. Humans had concocted any number of chemicals to kill plants on Earth. Those were the most common weapons Embassy Security found, Pyranz knew from lawsuits he'd prepared.

When Pyranz had first come to the planet, he had been surprised that anyone would want to kill plants. All plants had a purpose or the planet wouldn't have created them.

It made all Ruplovians doubt the reasons why the Unity High Council had decided to open an Embassy here. Then someone had discovered the massive insect population. Delicacies that none had ever tasted before and in abundance.

After going through security, Pyranz made his way through an airlock and then into the insect room for Levels 6 —8. It was humid and filled with growing plants and the best kind of light and soil. This was the largest room in the Embassy. Everyone needed to feed here in the fall, winter and early spring seasons.

Insects abounded and Pyranz only had to stand near a blooming *Brugmansia* and a tomato plant with rotting tomatoes before he caught six flies, a delicious bee and four mosquitos.

Not mosquitos who'd fed on blood though. Those were reserved for the lawyers. The top lawyers. Those in Levels 1 and 2.

Pyranz sealed the lid at the top of his tube. The insects

weren't weakened enough yet and he didn't want them to escape.

He left the room and went to his post. Switched on the artificial light above his workstation. He dug his feet into the damp soil. Relief. Even the feeding room hadn't given him enough water. He was seriously dehydrated.

Pyranz used his much-depleted credits to buy a sprinkling of water for his apartment. He'd turn it on after arriving home tonight, so he could get a good shower.

The day spun past. There were two new contracts to research.

One would supply humans hired to spend time in the mosquito room. Those mosquitos, once blood-filled, would then be transferred to the Level 1 and 2 insect room. The humans were well-compensated for this work and there was always a waiting list.

The other was for the Ruplovians to provide digestive sap to human drug companies. The sap was made into a drug called Rupidian which was given to human with digestive problems and lung ailments. The humans viewed it as a miracle drug.

Things seemed to work out well for everyone. To make sure there were no problems, and since these contracts covered new regions of Earth, research had to be done.

With the first contract, Pyranz came across the words servitude and slavery in his research. He felt something close to what humans would call shock, at what humans had done to other humans.

Humans seemed to have a tendency to divide themselves into groups and pit the groups against each other. These division lines made no sense too Pyranz. There was little order to them.

Some groups were regional. Others used different language groupings or gender groupings.

What they had in common was emotion, not logic. There were no real genus or species difference between the humans in these groups. The members of a group in power declared other groups as biologically inferior and things cascaded down from there.

There were divisions in Ruplovian society, but they were clear. Genetic testing on potential was done. There was solid data that Pyranz's brain would only develop so much. His abilities could only stretch so far. To put him in with the top lawyers and expect him to perform at Level 1 or 2 would be cruel. He was a solid Level 7.

His digestive acids would turn to water from the stress and he'd die of starvation. Now, he was being tested to the best of his ability. And he had *indigestion* as the humans would call it. Everyone had a finite range of development.

He could live with that. He had other gifts the top lawyers didn't. The tenacity to keep digging and digging into a subject until he found out everything. And the ability to filter out what was most pertinent to the project. Which made him invaluable as a researcher.

Pyranz could see from his research that humans were very sensitive about the words and concepts of servitude and labor. Understandable, given their history. Which meant the contract with the humans in the mosquito room had to be carefully worded. And it wasn't. The compensation wasn't clear.

If humans were paid well, their objections to certain work waned. Sometimes it even disappeared. Pyranz made a note of that on the contract. He included several words including: race, sex, gender, slavery, that were triggers for humans.

That would mean the contract would be rewritten and sent back to him for further approval. He sent it back.

Then he stretched in the artificial light and breathed deeply the moist air. Pyranz felt his tube feet suck up more moisture from the soil to nourish his body.

He settled into reading the other contract and added wordage to point out the human benefits of the contract.

Just then the entire system went down. As did the artificial lighting. Pyranz could still see. Ruplovians glowed in the dark.

He waited. There was a deadline on the contract which meant he needed to finish it today so it could work its way through the system.

Pyranz could feel the insect swarming around his tube. He kept the lid closed. Eventually they'd tire and fall into his digestive sap and drown.

Until then, the noise was deafening. The darkness continued.

Finally, one of the young clerks, a Level 2, came past and said, "Everyone go home. System down for today."

Pyranz dimmed in acknowledgement.

Nothing he could do about the contract. His home system wasn't integrated with the work one. It wouldn't have enough information to continue work at home. His level wasn't high enough for that.

He could do further work on his presentation. It was finished, but the alternative was to focus on the insects rumbling around in his tube. It was what humans referred to as an echo chamber.

By the time he got outside the Embassy, all the autovans were all filled up and gone. He'd need to take the train. With other beings.

Pyranz moved down the half block to the station. The

sidewalks were crowded and it was raining. Had the entire Embassy Hill shut down?

Rain or cold was fine with him. But the humans were bundled up and using umbrellas as if the rain would burn them.

He flashed an Embassy ID and the automated system let him through a gate to the train boarding area. It was outside, but in a covered area. He stood near the sign that read *Embassy Heights*.

The train was three minutes late. Pyranz used that time to watch the humans around him. His green skin was peppered with scarlet dots. Since his eyes were also scarlet, most beings couldn't easily see him staring at them.

There was a female with two young ones dancing around her. They didn't have gender signifiers on, as was the custom for youngsters. They got them at an age appropriate for their genus and species. For humans it was somewhere around eighteen. Pyranz couldn't remember the exact age. Eighteen and one-quarter? Seventeen and three-fourths?

The train came and he boarded, finding a place to lean between two dividers made to brace those who preferred to stand. The female and young humans sat across from him. The female carried many bags, as if she'd been shopping.

"Where are you from?" asked the tallest youngster.

"I'm from Ruplovia," Pyranz said politely.

It was not normal to speak to strangers. Not for Ruplovians or humans.

"Do they have Christmas on Ruplovia?" the child asked.

"Kirin," said the female, pulling on the child's sleeve.

"No, they do not. I am just learning about Christmas. Do you know a song called *The Twelve Days of Christmas?*"

The child began singing.

"On the first day of Christmas my true love gave to me a partridge in a pear tree.

On the second day of Christmas my true love gave to me two turtle doves and a partridge in a pear tree."

Then the other child and the female caretaker joined in.

"On the third day of Christmas my true love gave to me three French hens, two turtle doves and a partridge in a pear tree."

By the time they reached the end of the song, the entire coach had joined in the singing. Even though many beings stumbled over the words, everyone tried.

Pyranz even joined in on the last part. He didn't have a problem with knowing the words, but the pitch and sound of the words were difficult to get right. His voice had never been trained to sing.

There was no music on Ruplovia.

Pyranz opened his lid. He felt … something.

He didn't have a name for it, but it was an emotion. Ruplovians didn't feel emotions though. Not often.

All these strangers began to speak with each other. Beings from different planets throughout the multiverse conversed with each other and the humans.

Which never happened on trains. It had been the power of the song. A shared experience.

He would have to tell the group about it.

Pyranz got off at his stop, after thanking the children effusively for the song. The female caretaker beamed with pride.

Pyranz went to his apartment. Ruplovians were always housed on the lower floors of buildings. The structures were better reinforced to allow for the weight of damp soil.

He went through the first chamber and closed the outer door before opening the inner one to his room. Then dug his feet into the moistness and breathed in the earth air. After he'd settled, the insects began to fly around again.

Pyranz thought about trying to work from home, but none of the interfaces with the Embassy network would function. No, he'd work on his presentation.

Pyranz turned on the sprinkler system for the shower he'd bought earlier today. It didn't take long for the entire room to rehydrate. The soil seemed to breathe easier and he felt refreshed.

He had ideas about what to say, but what could he do to show the others what turtle doves were? He couldn't get hold of any real birds. They were endangered and didn't exist in this part of the world.

Pyranz didn't want to print any up like that huge blue Cassion who ate plants. He wouldn't stoop to copying her. He needed something different.

He would just have to try imaging.

Pyranz hadn't tried since he was a youngling. He'd failed badly. In front of all the other younglings. That had sealed his fate as a Level 7.

But he had no alternative.

Pyranz stood feeling his tube feet digging into the soil beneath them. Anchoring him to the floor of the building, which in turn was rooted in the soil of this alien planet. Here, alone in his apartment, he could be anything.

A sense of ease passed through him. Letting his juices and sap flow freely. He'd seen numerous photos of turtle doves. They were on the large size for Earth. About twenty-five centimeters long with a wingspan double that. But they were lean, not plump. A warm gray-brown color with white and black striped patches on the sides of their neck. The wing feathers were black, rimmed with a nutmeg color and the tail, black and white. The eyes, a darker nutmeg color with a black center.

Pyranz could easily see the bird in his mind, but it did not appear in the room in front of him.

His alarm pinged. It was time to leave for the study group.

He would just have to do what he did best. Show off his research skills. It would have to be enough.

Pyranz took an autovan to the meeting. The rain poured down. He didn't mind the walk to the building where the group met. The rain cleaned him nicely and felt refreshing.

Earth was a very good place for him. The water and air were clean. The soil full of nutrients. He could see himself living his entire life here. Ruplovians were long-lived. Without accidents, he could expect to live into his hundreds.

Humans could provide a fascinating research subject. They were a varied species. Even within their different subgroups diversity seemed endless. It was built into their species as a survival trait.

Pyranz stepped on the sensor in front of the door, which then opened. Inside the air was dry and warm. He moved down the corridor to the meeting room.

Niida, the Cassion and Martha, the Gassian were there already. Just as the previous two meetings.

Pyranz had decided they came early so that they could find enough space for their large bodies. Perhaps they didn't want to inconvenience others. Humans would have labeled that action kindness. Pyranz was coming to have much respect for humans, the more he researched them.

Perhaps he should extend that respect to the other members of this study group. He should learn more about them, too.

It was not the way of Ruplovians. However, he was no longer on Ruplovia.

"Good evening," he said.

"Hello," said Martha.

"Good evening," said Niida. "You're in a good mood tonight."

"Am I? Is that what it is called? I confess that Ruplovians don't understand emotions. We rarely feel them. But perhaps I am. Being on Earth is changing me."

"It is changing all of us," said Niida.

"I would like to talk to you about that sometime," said Pyranz.

Niida's tiny round ears fluttered. Pyranz didn't know what that meant.

"I'd like that," she said.

Then there was a flurry of noise as the other members of the study group arrived. Pyranz took his place at the front of the room, the chairs fanned out around him. He decided to stand for the presentation, just as he had when he'd once presented his findings to a group of Level 1's and 2's.

"Good evening," said Lula, their teacher. "Again, I'm Lula Pinnock, from Earth. Before we begin, I'd like everyone to go around and say their names and the planet they're from."

Pyranz knew all their names and home-worlds before they said them. Niida, the Cassion. Glitter, Blueberry, Tinkerbell, Mush and Shoe, the Meazza. Magwab, the Sartalan. Vert, the Camassan, another plant-based being. Squip, the Setagean. Asoona, the Tolpian. Daisy, the Catalpan. Renata and Jolie, the Duveilian. Kleep, the Tantoan. Schooos, the Ossian, who burned brightly tonight. And last Martha, the Gassian.

Pyranz bowed slightly, "I am Pyranz, from Ruplovia."

"Pyranz, you may begin your presentation.

Hello Everyone. Thank you for this opportunity. I have learned a lot by researching this presentation. My lyric is: *On the second day of Christmas my true love gave to me two turtle doves.* Turtle doves are a large-sized bird for Earth. About twenty-five centimeters long with a wingspan twice that. They are lean, not plump. Their body is a warm gray-brown color with white and black-striped patches on the sides of their necks. The wing feathers are black, rimmed with a nutmeg color and the tail, black and white. The eyes, a darker nutmeg color with a black center."

Pyranz heard someone say "Oooh."

There were other murmurs around the room.

Then he looked down and saw a pair of turtle doves on the ground in front of him. He had done it.

He had imaged. For the first time in his life.

He must keep his focus in order to maintain the full-dimensional images.

"They are quite beautiful birds and are endangered. They would have migrated to Africa in the fall and so would not have been in France, where the song probably originated, during Christmas. The turtle doves are mentioned in much human mythology from Greek to Christian. They pulled Aphrodite's chariot. She was the Greek Goddess of Love. They are much associated with love in human literature, especially in Shakespeare's plays. He made use of the fact that dove rhymes with love. The male, most likely, suitor in this song lyric was symbolically offering the female his love. He was also offering her food, since turtle doves were one of those species humans hunted nearly to extinction before giving them the official designation of endangered. Hunting and habitat loss nearly killed them all. That is all I've found about turtle doves, but I'd like to offer an observation about the song, if I may," said Pyranz.

The two turtle doves were walking around each other. Pyranz could hear their soft purring coo.

Lula said, "Please continue."

"I have a story to tell all of you. I left the Embassy early today. Our system went down and it seemed most of Embassy Hill had the same problem."

He heart murmuring and assents from the others.

"All the autovans were gone, so I took the train home. It was filled with many humans and other beings. Crowded and uncomfortable. Everyone out of their routine. Near me were two human youngsters and their female caretaker. One of the young ones asked me if we had Christmas on Ruplovia. I said no and asked the youngster if they knew this song. The child began singing it. The other young one joined in. Soon, the entire coach was singing. Beings who don't normally sing tried. There were many trying to learn or remember the correct words. Even if they didn't know the song, everyone sang. Even I made an attempt. After the song was finished, something very strange and unprecedented happened. Beings, complete strangers, began talking to each other. They conversed like old friends. It was the song, the shared experience of singing it or even listening to it that brought this on. Ruplovians don't make music. It is not part of our culture. But I actually felt something. I do not have a word for the emotion. Ruplovians rarely feel emotions and are not practiced at it. Our language has no words for emotions. We are beings of the mind. Some of the humans even were crying and smiling at the same time. This was a fascinating experience and I will be seeking out more music to see what effects it has on other people and myself."

Pyranz gave a small bow to indicate he was finished.

Everyone clapped and the two turtle doves took flight and disappeared. Pyranz felt something else. He couldn't name it either. But it was a pleasant feeling. Like when one's digestive sap is the perfect mix and there's the right mix of soil beneath one's feet and ample sunlight to grow in. Was it happiness?

Pyranz wasn't sure, but he intended to follow that feeling. And research further.

THREE FRENCH HENS

Martha spent the morning of her presentation running all over the Gassian Embassy. She was in charge of leading a group of seven and eight-year old humans and their teacher touring the Embassy.

This was her first tour she'd given alone. A day full of firsts.

Martha took a deep breath and willed her fur to turn blue, the color of balance. It turned a murky green color. As muddled as she felt.

The same two eight-year old boys had wandered off again. Martha left the teacher, whose name she couldn't remember, in charge of the rest of the group and went off to find them.

She finally discovered them in the Embassy kitchen, attempting to tie two of the cooks' tails together. Martha was tempted to bind the two of them up in the cleaning closet and leave them for security. But they weren't hers to deal with.

Instead, she grabbed each one by an ear, made a ferocious roaring sound as her fur turned red and hauled them back to the lobby.

She continued the tour for the others, while the teacher berated the two. The boys rubbed their ears. Martha didn't understand a lot about humans, but she did know that talking to the two boys wouldn't hinder them.

"Now this section of the Embassy is where the majority of our workers are."

She opened the door to a massive room filled with cushioned seats and Gassians conferencing together. Many were working alone at small tables pulled over the seats.

"Gassian seats are different from yours. They have no backs so there's ample room for our tails. And they're narrow at the front so we can straddle them with our two hind legs and still have a spot for our front leg. We pull our tables or desks to us over the seat."

"Where are your air-screens?" asked the teacher.

"We don't use them. They don't work well with our eyesight. We use solid screens on the tables," said Martha.

She pointed to the two boys who were sneaking off again.

The teacher grabbed both of them by the back of their shirts and dragged the two back to the tour.

"You two stay right in front of me," the teacher said, with a firm voice.

It seemed to take forever, but finally the tour was over and the children and teacher were all back on their train and gone. Martha plunked down on a seat in the lobby, her fur white. She was drained.

Her supervisor walked past, then backtracked and stood in front of her.

"Martha, go eat something. Now, before you collapse further."

Martha heaved herself up and had only moved one step towards the feeding area, when one of the cooks gave a high-pitched whistle. The door to the workroom flew open and there was a thundering sound of hundreds of feet as everyone ran to the food room.

Martha sat back down. Her supervisor was gone. Joined in with the rest.

She couldn't deal with the jostling for food. Not today. Maybe she should just go down the street to one of the human eating areas. She'd need to order five meals though.

Martha checked her credits. Her account was low. Mostly from the expenses for the presentation. But there was enough to squeak through till she earned more credits.

She checked out at the Embassy door and walked down the street. It was raining again. Hard. Her fur would shed some of the water, but she'd still be wet. The gardenia scent would become overpowering. Which meant she'd need to shower and dry herself before the meeting tonight.

She should probably wear the waterproof coat she'd been been given by the Embassy upon arrival at this post. So as not to offend other beings with sensitive noses. But it was so uncomfortable. Still, she'd wear it tonight.

Tonight was special. Martha wanted to make a good impression with her presentation.

After a lunch of ten beef and bean burritos, Martha felt herself again. She walked back into the Embassy and stood for a time in the lobby beneath the cool blowers, drying her fur. The cold air felt just perfect.

The afternoon was spent gathering supplies for a new project hospitality was planning. They were presenting an evening of Gassian History to a group from various embassies next week. By the time the day ended Martha was nearly white again.

She went to the feeding room and ate some leftover stoosh and woolp. The small herbivore's meat was rubbery from being reheated and the woolp had dissolved into a mushy paste. Those leaves should never be cooked. The Embassy cooks were having a bad day, too.

After eating, her fur darkened to a a green color. Perhaps at home she'd find some calm.

Martha was on the first autovan to the Gassian Plains, where the newer Embassy employees were housed. It was farther from the Embassy than the Gassian Towers. But employees didn't get to move into the Towers until someone higher-up left the city for another post, or died. She'd be living at the Plains for a very long time. Gassians loved New Seattle.

The trip through the city was dimly lit inside the van. The sun had already set. Outside the city glistened like a jewel with all the colored lights and rain pooling everywhere.

The autovans, busses and trains had helped ease traffic problems in the city, but not enough. It took two hours to get home. No time for a shower.

She scheduled a van pick-up and stood under the cold blower, drying her fur as best she could. She was in deep meditation when it turned off. Her fur was blue again.

She ate a quick snack of three boxes of powdered sugar doughnuts, brushing the white sugar off of her fur. Then slipped on the waterproof coat and went down to the lobby to wait for the van.

It was late. Martha hoped the human she'd hired was on schedule. It wouldn't be good if they were late for her presentation.

Finally the autovan arrived.

"I am so sorry for the lateness. Traffic is terrible tonight," said the AI system.

Martha didn't reply. She got in and strapped herself in. She couldn't make the straps large enough around her waist, so just settled for the upper body safety straps.

The van took off with a jolt and sped towards the Firs at Douglas Creek, where the study group met. Traffic was still jammed. On the freeway and in the air. She couldn't afford a flying car or van, but there were many who could.

The autovan finally passed an accident that had been clogging up traffic. The bots hadn't gotten there to pick up the vehicles, but ambulances were flying away with passengers. One of the vehicles was an old human-driven one. A little purple sporty car. Probably caused the problem. Human-driven vehicles should be illegal.

After that they moved along at a good speed. Martha breathed easier. With luck, she'd get to the meeting on time. At least she wouldn't have to worry about where to sit. She'd be in the speaker's position.

She closed her eyes, trying once again to find calm. It wouldn't be good if her fur was purple or green throughout the entire presentation. She focused on the color yellow, but would settle for blue.

It was still raining heavily by the time the van arrived at the destination. Martha was pleased she'd worn the raincoat.

At least her smell wouldn't be as strong. Some beings loved the scent, humans called it a gardenia smell. Martha felt sure just as many beings despised it, but politely said nothing. When she didn't shower often enough it overwhelmed even her. And she'd badly needed a shower this evening.

Well, nothing she could do about that. She got out of the van and walked into the building. As soon as Martha got inside, she shed the raincoat, shaking it and hanging it on a hook in the hallway. Nearly everyone was there.

Including a strange human with a large box, covered with a thick white cloth. She must be the one Martha had hired.

Martha went over to the woman, who was speaking with Lula.

"Hello, I'm Martha. Are you Dia?"

"I am. Good, I was hoping this was the right place. I don't know the city much. Where should I put this?" Dia asked, pointing at the box.

"Right up in the front. You can put it in front of the chair. I won't be using the chair," said Martha.

"Okay. Do you want me to leave during your talk?"

"No, you're welcome to stay," said Martha.

She wanted Dia around, just in case there was a problem.

Dia lifted the box as if it weighed nothing. Squawking noises emerged from the box as she balanced it on her shoulder. The woman walked between two empty chairs and set the box down in the front of the chair at the front. Then Dia sat in an empty chair in the second row back.

Martha sat in front, near the box. Inside she could hear soft clucking noises. She waited for everyone to arrive and Lula to begin the group.

Ironically, Kleep was one of the late ones and apologized three times to everyone for their lateness. Tantoans detested tardiness by anyone. Apparently, there was more than one accident on the roads tonight.

Vert was the last to arrive. She seemed mortified, slinking to a seat, his fronds a pale green.

Lula stood up and said, "Welcome everyone. I'd like to

introduce our visitor, Dia. She brought something for Martha's presentation. I'd like to let you know that the human Christmas shopping season has begun. There will be more people and vehicles out on the road until Christmas. Humans searching for gifts. Many people shop after work, going out to eat, instead of dining at home. Restaurants and cafes will be more crowded. There will be more accidents and more rain. So take that into consideration and if you can start out for this group earlier than normal. And if it snows, just stay home. Even the autovans aren't prepared for travel on our slippery hills. We'll reschedule the group for another time. But tonight, Martha's going to talk about the Third Day of Christmas."

Lula sat back down and looked at Martha.

"Good evening," said Martha.

She didn't stand, not wanting to tower over most everyone.

"My lyric to present is: *On the third day of Christmas, my true love gave to me three French hens*. This song has gone through many variations. In some versions it has been three fat hens, in others three foreign hens. French hens were a delicacy and several breeds were exported to other countries around the Earth," said Martha, pulling the cloth off the box and revealing a wire cage containing three white chickens.

They had small red fleshy protrusions on their chins and above their beaks. The birds rose, flapped their wings and squawked a few times before settling down and peering out at the audience.

Martha continued, "These birds are a breed called *Bresse Gaulois*. They became popular in early France along with several other breeds. These chickens are a good example of what our suitor would have given his true love. Besides being the queen of poultry, and a good meal, the hens also lay eggs. Meaning more chickens or simply eggs to eat. And white chickens were a symbol of good luck. Does anyone have any questions?" asked Martha.

"Can we let them out?" asked Squip.

"No," said Lula. "None of us want to pay to have this room deep cleaned.

A look of relief passed over Dia's face. Martha felt the same way.

She also noticed her fur was blue. Good.

"Can I eat one?" asked Magwab.

"No, you must go buy chicken at a restaurant or grocery store like other beings. These chickens are Dia's pets. She breeds them and shows them."

"What does that mean?" asked Vert, who seemed to have greened up as the meeting progressed.

Martha looked at Dia.

Dia stood and said, "I let the hens run with a rooster. Roosters are the male birds, hens the female. The hens lay eggs that are fertilized and then hatch out into baby chickens. Those with perfect characteristics of the breed are chosen as show birds. The others I sell on to those who simply want to raise birds for their eggs or sometimes for meat. These are not actually *Bresse Gaulois*, but *American Bresse* since they live in this country. They cannot legally be called *Bresse Gaulois* simply because they don't reside in France. They have the same breed requirements though. Chickens generally are short-lived. If I'm lucky, these gals will live 10-12 years. These girls are two years old right now. I take them to shows where they are compared to other chickens, brought by other breeders, to decide which chicken exemplifies the best of that breed. If I win it makes my chickens worth more, as well as my baby chicks that someone might buy to raise up."

"Do humans normally show chickens?" asked Daisy.

"No, it is heritage work. Keeping alive ancient breeds. The same with heirloom plants and crafts. It is our past, our history. We have lost so much of our world with the swift rise of technology. Some of us have chosen to preserve what we can in this modern world."

"And the rest of us thank you for it," said Lula.

Martha beamed. Her presentation was going well.

Dia was asked more questions. Some of the group came up to look more closely at the hens. Some of the beings had never seen a real live bird, up close.

At the end of her presentation, everyone clapped. Martha's fur remained blue the entire presentation.

At the end, everyone sat down again. Lula stood and walked to the center of the room, standing beside Martha.

"I hope all of you are working on your presentations. Are any of you having problems?" asked Lula.

Glitter wildly waved a thin black arm.

"Glitter," said Lula.

"We cannot find anything about pipers."

"Look under music. Pipers played musical instruments."

"We will try that," said Shoe, as the five Meazza stood on their chair and turned inward, having a quick conference with each other.

"I found many types of lords. Which does the song lyric concern?" asked Magwab.

"Nobility. French and English. Look back into the history of those countries," said Lula. "Any more questions?"

The room was silent except for the murmur of the hens.

"Our next meeting, Schooos will present. See you then," said Lula.

Martha felt relieved. She put the cloth back over the hens' box. Then paid Dia her final payment, transferring the credits to Dia's account.

Dia held out her right hand and Martha shook it, remembering the curious human custom.

"Pleasure doing business with you," said Dia.

"And you too," said Martha.

Dia picked up the box and left the room, walking towards the entrance. She was unlike any human Martha had met. Most of the humans she had dealt with were either touring the Embassy, like the children and their teacher today or doing business there.

Dia was someone else entirely. Tall and strong, she carried herself with a sort of power that most humans didn't have. Dia knew where she belonged in the multiverse and she inhabited her place fully. Martha admired her for that.

Martha longed for the type of certainty that Gassians generally achieved through age. Although there were some her age who had that confidence.

Martha decided she would be one of them. She would remember this day. When she'd gone from ineptly herding human children around to giving her presentation to a room full of other beings, all of them nearly strangers.

Her fur was still blue.

Martha left the building, after being congratulated by Lula, Niida and Pyranz. She carried the raincoat, not worried about getting her fur wet now.

She got into the autovan to return to the Gassian Plains. By the time, Martha reached home, her fur was yellow. A blissful yellow color that showed how at peace she was with herself.

Her fur had never, ever, been yellow.

Martha strode through the common area and lobby to her apartment. Her fur still yellow. She knew people were staring, including her supervisor.

Now that Martha had achieved yellow, she knew how to do it again. She could replicate this feeling.

Tranquility belonged to her.

In her rooms, Martha took a long shower, then blew her fur dry. As she drifted off to sleep, Martha looked forward to a long yellow day tomorrow. And the day after. And the day after that.

FOUR CALLING BIRDS

I GOT THE MORNING INFLUX OF FRESH GASES WHICH FANNED my flames, increasing the heat in my own room. Then stretched, reveling in the freedom of not wearing the suit. All the Ossian residences were lined with tungsten, so the walls wouldn't burn.

I loved the subtle color of the mineral. A soft warm gray color which felt inviting. It made me think of the caves of Ossia, where I was born.

Those caves were made of a different mineral. We Ossians don't even have a single word from it. Its name would comprise an entire book for humans. The name describes every property and known use the mineral contains.

Just as my name does. We Ossians live very long lives and take the time to name things and beings properly. Upon my arrival on Earth, I shortened my name to Schooos Gal Mantobiane de Forgemalla. Most humans call me Schooos.

I breathed in more of the fresh gases, adding a bit more oxygen to the mix to prepare for going out into the world. It felt blissful. I let the sweet scent of methane, propane and hydrogen fill my senses.

It felt so indulgent to be without my suit. The suits were so restrictive, but that was the price we Ossians paid for seeing the multiverse.

And I wasn't regretting it. I loved meeting the variety of beings who existed on Earth. Even if I didn't always understand them. Which was why I'd been chosen as a public relations officer for the Ossian Embassy.

And why I'd signed up for this study group. To speak with others in a non-official capacity.

I hadn't planned on needing to give an entire presentation. I didn't feel confident that people could understand me. Or that what I had to say would be interesting to them.

We Ossians find everything interesting, even down to the minutest detail. Other beings, often do not.

I had to give my presentation tomorrow and all my preparation so far consisted of voice work. Trying to overcome the hissing of the speakers in my suit. They needed to be replaced, but I was at the end of the list. I would have to do without until then.

It was my own fault. Upon first arriving on Earth, I had fried the speakers too often with my exuberance at meeting so many new beings. I have since gotten more experience at lowering my flames.

I could overcome the hiss during my work day, but this was different. A presentation in a large room with so many smooth surfaces. There was a lot of echo in that room.

All of which meant, I'd done no research for my presentation. I would do it today during my break. Human history wasn't that detailed, not compared to the Ossian past.

Tonight, there was a gathering downstairs at the Furnace.

Which was what the Ossian residence was called. I was looking forward to it. I had missed the last one, it had been scheduled the same night as the study group.

Reluctantly, I pulled the metal and synthetic suit over my flames, lowering them so as not to overheat the suit. I sealed it completely, so no heat or gases could escape. The faceplate steamed up for a bit, then cleared. As was normal.

I stepped out of my room and closed the door. Then moved down the corridor to the air tube that took me to the main floor. I stepped off the floor into the downstream flow and was floated through the air sinking to the lobby.

I caught the second autovan, the first was already full. Most all Ossians left for the Embassy at the same time.

The van was mostly quiet, all of us doing our morning meditation. The AI was its usual cheerful self. Whoever had programmed it seemed to believe that talking was essential to put the passengers to rest.

When I heard humans talking about morning autovans, it was always with derision. They just wanted the AI to shut up.

I found the patter of its language a pleasant background. Especially mixed with the pounding rain.

The water was coming down so hard. I looked out the moisture-streaked windows of the autovan onto darkness and headlights. It was a lovely contrast. Like a painting of that human, what was his name? Monet? Van Gogh? I couldn't be sure who the painter was.

I stopped searching and simply enjoyed the painting as it rolled past my window. My own visual meditation.

The morning at the Embassy was filled with problems. The Duveilian contingent complaining about a missing Ossian gas shipment that they'd been billed for. I channeled that to billing to solve. Then the Tolpian representative wanting to know when their shipment of Galatinatti would arrive. I sent them to the trade specialists.

Galatinatti is one of the main exports of Ossia. A precious gemstone, so far only found on Ossia. It contains all the colors in existence and shimmers with each one individually, according to the heat and light it is exposed to. It can take very high heat, but only an Ossian wearing one can make the stones shine the deep clear blue of an Ossian lake. An Ossian without a suit. I planned to wear mine tonight for the gathering.

It was a rather large jewel, passed down through my family. I received it when I came of age at sixty. I would give it to my new division, if ever that young one came to be. That was many, many human lifetimes from now.

After solving half a dozen other problems, I took my break and went into a back room to use a screen.

There was more information on the song than I expected to find, but only some of it applied to my assigned day. Most of it was about the later, more complex lyrics.

The original lyric was *Four colly birds*. Which meant coal-black birds. Then it was changed to canary, which meant colored. Then collie. Then curley and coulored. One version switched it completely to ducks. Then it reverted to colly and collie. In a later version it was changed to calling birds.

Blackbirds were considered food at the time of the song. Mostly for the lower classes.

I only have a slight understanding of human class systems of the past. I'd thought the song was about a middle or upper-class couple.

Then I read on about humans baking live blackbirds into pies. What an awful thing to do. Humans were a still-barbaric group who had barely qualified for Unity membership. They had a ways to go yet before their civilization left things like this in the distant past.

So, like the previous lyrics, the lover was giving the loved one food. Which for humans symbolized abundance.

I still had to struggle to make the connection that other beings on this planet were considered food for humans. I felt relief at being Ossian. Who lived solely on gases. And returned other gases, such as oxygen in exchange.

After doing more research, I returned to the front entryway to direct beings entering the Embassy. It was a busy afternoon. More than once I had to remind myself to dim my flames to keep from damaging my suit.

And then the work day was over. I raced for the auto van, eager for the evening to begin.

Back at my home, I shed the suit, hanging it upon the hook. I breathed in the nutritive gases and adorned myself with my galitinatti, hung on a chain of pure silensiana. The jewel shimmered a deep purple, but not the clear blue. That would come later.

I felt wonderful. It was time.

I took the air tube and caught the downstream to the lobby. Others were ahead of me and behind as well. I could feel the energy, the anticipation of everyone. Even before entering the gathering room.

The room felt quite full tonight. Often, Ossians had oblig-ations and couldn't attend. Not so tonight. This gathering would bring together the vitality of many.

We stood, flame touching flame. Waiting for everyone to arrive and the doors closing, so as not to damage anything in the lobby.

Back on Ossia, the gatherings took place in deep caves

and the shared power nurtured those not in attendance as it diminished and drifted through the cave systems.

Finally, the doors closed and we all stood as equals. The room shone with our combined brilliance.

Humans would have found the light blinding and the heat would have burned them.

We breathed in and out, allowing the boundaries of our individual flames to loosen, until we became one burning mass. Sharing thought, sharing feeling, sharing everything.

Within the gathering one completely loses sense of time. There is no today, yesterday or tomorrow. There is only now.

Our flames and bodies melded together, losing all form. Becoming one flame. My jewel, shared by all, just as I shared whatever the others had worn.

As the gathering went on, the heat in the room increased. In the very center of the room lay a pile of fire rock, brought from Ossia. Within the fire rock lay a large chunk of carbon. When the heat and pressure from the gather became strong enough, the fire rock exploded. Littering chunks of diamond around the room. That is our signal the gather has ended.

Tonight, it felt like years had passed before the diamonds and fire rock began to pelt us and as we withdrew back into our individual bodies, the deep gaseous sound of spontaneous laughter filling the room.

Laughter only happened after the most satisfying gathers.

We lowered our flames and collected the diamonds, putting them into a container. They would be sold and the credits used to pay for our living expenses. Ossian diamonds were a sought-after rarity and demanded high prices.

The fire rock was collected to be taken to the basement. Where moisture, pressure and cool temperatures would make it congeal so it could be reused at a future gather.

Once we had collected all the stones, the vacuums would do the rest. Sucking up and sorting the tiniest pieces.

We all left the room, closing the doors behind us so the vacuums could do their work. Then took the air tube up to our various rooms.

The air stream going up was red with fire all the way to the top of the building. A beautiful sight.

I got off on my floor and returned to my room. Feeling refreshed and refilled. At one with all Ossianity.

My lovely jewel glowed a deep clear blue. It mirrored the lakes of my youth. I gave a deep sigh. Those had been peaceful days, even if they'd been long, long ago.

The next day that blissful energetic feeling still remained. I would have a good day and a wonderful presentation.

I went about my day at the Embassy, confined in the suit. Not losing control of my flames.

I felt compassion for the human diamond merchant, who didn't have quite enough money to purchase the last batch of our diamonds. Even when he tried to bribe me to steal some for him.

Ossians are beyond bribery or theft. We have everything we desire provided for us. We are very fortunate.

I helped the Setagean Delegation understand what our world is like. They are touring various embassies to gain a better understanding of the multiverse.

When the day was finished, I returned home for a couple of hours. Removed my suit and refreshed myself. Then put it back on and took the autovan through the downpour of rain, to the group.

I sat on the chair at the front of the room. Niida, Martha and Magwab were rearranging the chairs when I arrived.

I sat and prepared myself to give my presentation. I let

my suit release certain gases and formed them into a tight ball in front of me, keeping anyone from breathing something which might harm them.

They closed the curtains at my request and dimmed the lights, then took their seats. The other members of the group arrived and sat.

Lula got up and said, "Tonight, we have Schooos presenting the fourth day of Christmas. Take it away Schooos."

I remained seated and spoke, working to diminish the hiss of my speakers. "Good evening. I hope all of you are well. The lyric for the fourth day of Christmas is very straightforward. *On the fourth day of Christmas, my true love gave to me four colly birds.* The song has changed throughout time. It began as colly birds. Which was a term that meant coal-black birds. It is thought the song referred to blackbirds, rather than crows or ravens. Blackbirds were commonly eaten at that time, mainly by the lower-classes. They were also baked into pies for the upper-class. The word was later changed to canary, which meant colored. Then curley, then coloured. It went back and forth, even being changed to ducks. Then was switched to calling birds. In the most-recent versions it has returned to colly birds. The suitor was giving his intended a meal, or perhaps four. Perhaps thirty-two if that gift truly was repeated for the next eight days as the song indicates. Food is clearly love to this suitor, proving he can give her the essence of life."

While speaking I used my power, dimmed by the confining suit, to project images in the space in front of where I sat.

I made the gases form blackbirds, crows and ravens. Then blackbirds again. Then a pie with live birds bursting through the crust. Then colored birds, followed by white ducks. Then the suitor and his love. Then four blackbirds who changed into thirty-two.

The room gasped at the images moving through the room around them. The creation looked thin to me, but was the best I could do while wearing a suit.

"That is all I could find on my lyric," I said.

I moved the gases back into a ball, making sure none escaped. Then sucked them back into my suit, through the intake system.

Lula stood and clapped. The others joined her.

Magwab switched the lights back on.

"That was wonderful, Schooos. I've never seen anything like it. It was like a painting or a sculpture that continually reformed. Beautiful! All of your presentations have been enlightening and creative beyond my expectations. I'm so excited to see what the rest of you come up with."

I felt relieved my words had been understood. I only wished I could have conveyed to them all the joy of a gathering.

To be able to share that would be to bring the multiverse together.

But some things are beyond words.

FIVE GOLDEN RINGS

Kleep perched on the large cushioned desk chair in the lobby of the Tantoan Embassy. Through the large armored glass windows they could see it was blustery outside. Other being's belongings blew sideways through the rain-drenched wind.

Ci shoved their other two bodies over to get more room so Ar could see the screen. It was a slow day, enabling them to do continue researching for the study group presentation. At least until the receptionist returned from their lunch break.

The sliding door shooshed open and a group of humans came in. The speaker walked to the desk and said, "Hello, I'm Kiri Hanssen. We're here for a training."

Ci switched the screen to reservations. Ar looked at the screen.

The humans were scheduled at 12:00 p.m., not 1:00 p.m. as Kleep had been told. Panic rushed through them. It would not do for a Tantoan to be late. They hated such rudeness.

And humans were almost always late. Well, it was 12:01 p.m., so technically, the humans were late.

Bu said, "If you will be seated, we will be with you shortly."

The human nodded and returned to the others.

Ci's slender black fingers tapped out a message to the receptionist.

Must go give a presentation now. Cut your lunch break short.

There was a response, which Ar read. The receptionist was on their way back.

Kleep lowered the chair and slid off. Then Ci walked them over to the humans.

"If you would follow us," said Bu.

They walked down the left corridor to the fourth meeting room. Bu spoke to the AI system.

"Lights and screen please."

The room lit up and the full-wall screen appeared at the end of the room.

The humans took seats in the semi-circle of chairs at the other end of the small room. Kleep remained standing. Letting the humans get a good look at them. Finally, the humans had stowed their bags and other belongings and were ready to pay attention.

"We are Kleep," said Bu. "We will be giving your presentation today. We have been told that your are from the Axion Corporation, are we correct?"

"Yes," said a tall woman.

At least she looked tall, but humans were generally a couple meters taller than Tantoans. This one looked more like three meters taller.

"The Tantoan Embassy is one of the newest embassies to open in New Seattle, although we have been with the Unity for over a hundred of your Earth years. We realize that humans are unfamiliar with us, so we will start at the beginning.

"Although you see what appears to be three separate bodies in front of you, we are one connected being. Ar is female, she controls our sight."

Ci made Ar wave her arm.

"Ci is intersex and controls our movement."

Ci waved an arm.

"I am Bu, male, and I control our sound."

Ci made Bu wave his hand.

"All together we are Kleep. We are totally dependent on each other and one body cannot survive the death of any other body. Which is why we have armored limbs, torsos and heads.We are completely connected in ways that humans cannot see. We think and feel as one.

"I know that many humans view us a repulsive. Some have even said we resemble what you call stick insects. Even though we are much larger than any insect on Earth. Our culture is much older than any human culture, and more advanced. As you can see from the screen behind us, Tantoans exist in many colors and our bodies are varied," Ci gestured at the screen, which was showing photos of the great diversity of Tantoan body types.

"We are not your giant horror movie insects." Ci tilted all their heads to the right to indicate a joke.

The humans laughed nervously and shuffled in their seats.

"We Tantoans are all alike in that we each have three bodies. Three is a significant number for us. A sacred number. Humans have tried to understand how our culture works and we struggle to explain it to them. You do not have words in your language that allow us to easily express the concepts which make our world tick, to borrow a human phrase.

"We are highly regulated, from within our own beings. Not from without, as many Earth cultures have been. We're keenly aware of time. To be late is a terrible insult for us. It keeps others waiting, which we find unbearably rude. But it also delays forward progress. When a meeting begins late, things begin to fall apart.

"The Tantoan brain is marvelously complex—as it must be to move three bodies when only one is coordinating them, to make three bodies speak when only one has the ability or send visual input to three minds to see when only one has eyesight. And every Tantoan is always having a three-way internal conversation happening as they go through inter-acting with the outside world. Each one connected to the others, yet somewhat independent. Tantoans make up some of the most advanced scientists, mathematicians and thinkers in the entire multiverse."

Slides of famous Tantoans and their achievements slid across the screen behind them. Kleep paused for a few moment, so the humans could take them in.

"It may take three of us to move through the world and interact physically with it, but our minds are separate, yet connected. Kleep is quite capable of living without any other beings. The stimulation of our mind keeps us entertained. Yet, to do so would be selfish. We have much to share with the world.

"Tantoa's main exports are our citizens. We happily share our knowledge and expertise with other worlds. We do export many sought after and rare minerals, as our system is filled with meteors and small planets laden with such.They are, what you humans would call, paying the bills. But our minds, those are the real treasures.

"We know that Axion Corporation is primarily interested in importing our rare minerals. We are pleased to work with you. Does anyone have questions?" asked Bu.

"If I'm working with a particular Tantoan and can't contact them, can someone else do their job?" asked a man with facial hair on his chin. "I've had that problem with other embassies."

"If you can't contact them, then something is wrong. Contact our embassy and we'll look into it. We Tantoans are punctual, cooperative and generally available. To ignore someone who one is doing business with is simply rude and incompetent. There have been a few kidnappings of various embassy members of late, I'm sure you're aware of that. The Free Earth Movement has not been bothered with Tantoans at this point, but we would ask you to let us know if your contact is not responding. It might be an emergency."

"Is it true that Tantoans don't have possessions? asked a short man with no hair on the top of his head.

Which must be by choice. Humans had many means to put hair wherever they wished.

"Tantoans don't value possessions. Our minds are our most precious possessions. As well as our lives. We simply see no need. We don't wear clothes like humans. There is no such thing as fashion. Our only ornamentation is gender indicators, for beings who need to see such things. We live communally in a large common room. Individual sleeping chambers are available and when we leave, they are auto cleaned for the next Tantoan. We have embassy vehicles to use, but mostly travel by auto vans. Everything we need is provided for.

Possessions are irrelevant. We admit that other beings desire for possessions is puzzling."

Ar looked around the room.

A woman with short hair stood.

"What else would Tantoans consider rude or offensive?" the human asked. Then sat down.

"Well, we admire punctuality and precision, especially in ourselves. We do our best to try not to take offense where it isn't intended. We dislike those who are ill-prepared for a meeting. If you're negotiating a shipment of mineral imports, we suggest you have all the information ready. Most professional business-people are not doing anything offensive. Tantoan rules are much the same as yours. We would say that you should stay within the bounds of propriety. Cheating a business partner would be foolish. You will not get a second chance. We Tantoans work for mutually beneficial solutions. It took us a very long time and much suffering to learn that this is always the best way to act."

Ar looked around the room. There seemed to be no more questions.

"Shall we take a tour of the public areas of our Embassy?"

"Yes," murmured some of the humans.

"Follow me," said Bu.

Bu led them through the main work room, where most of the work was done. Contracts being written, mineral shipments tracked and the communications center with Tantoa.

The map room was always popular. The humans could walk around planets and meteors projected onto a massive dome. They could zoom into areas with the minerals they were interested in. Humans were very tactile beings Kleep had found.

Keen buyers knew exactly which regions they wanted to import materials from. There were always slight regional differences, although few of them were measurable by unsophisticated human equipment.

Bu was able to hone in on the largest city on Tantoa and the government offices there. To show the great central marketplace at its busiest and the grand ballroom where Tantoan gathered for elaborate dances.

Altogether, the tour took up the rest of the afternoon. Kleep never did get lunch. Or have time to do more research and come up with a solution for the presentation.

Kleep conferred amongst themselves all the way home.

What shall we do for our presentation? Ar rolled her eyes.

There isn't much information about what that silly song lyric could mean. Bu coughed.

Not beyond the two things. Everyone else has brought birds in some manner or another. Let's present the other interpretation we came up with. Ci raised two arms in the gesture of emphasis.

What you proposed would be immoral. Ar blinked.

They are not our partners. We have no contract with them. We are not bound by the normal restrictions. Bu laughed.

Well?

Ar conceded. *You are right. Yes then.*

Good. Tonight? Ci drummed long slender fingers on the van seat.

You have it all planned don't you? Bu clicked his tongue.

Not completely. Ci raised two hands, the sign of resignation. *I need some supplies. And a little more research.*

Tomorrow then. Ar closed her eyes.

Tomorrow. Bu let out a deep sigh.

Agreed. Tomorrow. Everything will be ready. Ci sat back against the van seat. Smiling.

The next morning sped past. At lunchtime, Kleep left the building as they'd planned.

Kleep had taken the afternoon off, requesting use of an Embassy autocar. One of the small, nondescript ones, which blended in with other cars in the city. The license plate had no number. Simply the logo of the Tantoan Embassy. One of many in use at that time of day. Kleep also arranged that there would be no record of who used the car and disabled its tracking system.

That happened at embassies more than beings would think. It would go unnoticed.

Traffic was busy in the shopping district of New Seattle. Sheets of rain gushed down. Tantoans weren't fond of the rain, but humans were a long way from mastering climate control. Other Unity members couldn't interfere, much as they wished too.

Kleep had the car stop and park on the main street, just outside their destination. Stephenson's Jewelers. They waited until a well-dressed human in a gray overcoat and hat went into the busy store.

Then Kleep went inside, trying to ignore the unpleasant wetness on their exoskeleton. The door opened automatically once all three of them were on the pad.

"Remember this for the way out," said Bu.

Kleep pretended to look in several metal and glass columnar cases, until the man in gray had been waited on. The salesclerk, an old man with white thinning hair and thick eyeglasses, took out a tray and set it on top of the old glass counter for the man to inspect.

The man in gray picked up one gold ring and moved slightly to the left of the tray, as if to inspect the ring more closely.

"What is this decoration supposed to be?" he asked the clerk, handing him the ring.

The clerk took it and looked closely, then snapped the magnifier attached to his glasses down.

Kleep was already in place. Ci reached up next to the man in gray and snagged six rings. Just in case one wasn't gold. Ci shoved them into a small bag strapped around the waist and continued looking along the counters on the way out the door. Then Ci got them all on the pad and the door opened. They were out.

Kleep ran for the car and took off. There was no doubt the cameras had caught it all, but they had the diplomatic car. And all Tantoans looked alike to humans. Plus they had diplomatic immunity.

"Will he talk?" asked Bu.

He's been well paid. The last credits are now winging their way to his account. He will not be suspected, because they will see us on their cameras. It will all work out as planned. Ci smiled.

Kleep had the car take them straight to the living quarters and park. They would ride in it to the study group.

Kleep continued to do research and they went over their presentation until it was time to eat with the early shift. The brined carpata was especially fine, tangy and salty.

Following the meal, they piled into the embassy car and went to the study group. Lula had been correct. Traffic was even worse tonight than it had been for the previous group. The combination of darkness, rain and too many beings on the roads was terrible. And there were still far too many humans not using auto cars.

Kleep couldn't imagine the not-so distant past where all cars were driven by humans. Far more accidents and much worse traffic. Even with less beings on Earth.

Kleep had plenty of time to see that they had five gold rings and one white-gold. Would that count as gold for the song? Maybe not. Ci put that one in a different compartment of the bag.

Still, they arrived early, even with the traffic.

Martha and Niida were already there, sitting beside each other talking. Kleep took the chair at the front of the room, all of them perching on it.

"Good evening," said Martha.

"A very good evening to both of you," said Bu.

"Do you need anything for your presentation?" asked Niida.

"We have everything we need. Thank you," said Bu.

Eventually, everyone was there. Only Lula was late, as usual.

"Good evening everyone," she said. "Sorry I'm late. There was a bad accident on the freeway. All lanes except one were closed."

She shook off her raincoat, draping it over an empty chair.

Then said, "Kleep, what do you have for us tonight on Day 5?"

"Kleep looked long and hard for complexities on this lyric, but there were few. It is not a deeply symbolic verse. *On the fifth day of Christmas my true love gave to me five golden rings,* is sometimes said to refer to goldfinches or goldspinks as they were called. Other people say it refers to ring-necked pheasants which were thought to have gold rings around their necks, but don't. Goldfinches were kept as caged birds, presumably for their songs. Pheasants were eaten, as were many of the other birds in the song. Kleep has decided that the intended had probably got enough food and that the lover turned to more convincing gifts. Gold rings are symbolic of commitment for humans. They are meant to tell the intended that the lover is serious.

"We have brought a replica of such rings."

Ci pulled the rings out of their bag and handed the five rings to Daisy to pass around.

"These are real gold?" asked Asoona.

"Yes, they are," said Bu.

"Where did you get them?" asked Glitter. "I though Tantoans had no possessions."

"They are on loan," said Bu.

"Beautiful," said Squip, handing them to Renata/Jolie.

She wiped the slime off of the rings before passing them on.

"That is all we could find on our lyric."

"That's just fine," said Lula. "Some lyrics are richer than others. Oh, these are lovely. Look at the fine work on this one. Vines all wrapped around each other."

Lula passed the rings back to Kleep just as the door burst open and four humans in dark blue walked in.

The one in the lead, headed right for Kleep.

"Can I help you gentlemen?" asked Lula, in a voice sterner than Kleep's first intermediate level master.

"Let me see those rings," said the man in the lead, his voice deep.

"Certainly," said Bu.

Ci handed the man the five rings.

"Where did you get these?"

"As a member of the Tantoan Embassy, we are not required to answer your question. Although we will. These rings came from Stephenson's Jewelers."

"There's one missing."

Ci pulled the sixth ring out of the small bag and handed it to the man.

"So you stole them," said the man, his neck and face reddening. A sign of anger for humans, Kleep noted.

"No. You misunderstand our intent and actions. We required them for our presentation tonight. So everyone could learn. They would have been returned when the store opens again tomorrow."

"You committed a crime."

"We have diplomatic immunity," said Bu

Ci flashed Bu's palm and lit up the Embassy Stamp contained within it.

One of the other darkly-dressed humans came up to confer with the belligerent one. Lula also joined into their discussion.

Kleep couldn't hear everything said, but did catch Lula's words.

"You're in a room full of representatives from twelve different embassies. I don't think you want to make this an incident, do you?"

The two strangers turned to look around the room. The man's face changed as understanding came to him.

"I think we can say this was a misunderstanding. The rings have been recovered," said the strange woman.

"I will do my best to explain what has gone wrong here," said Lula.

The man shrugged his shoulders. "Not much else we can do here."

As they left, the man glared rudely at Kleep. They pretended not to see him.

"I know this was an unintended error, but in the future I would advise all of you to stay within human laws in acquiring your presentation materials," said Lula. "Well, that was certainly exciting, Kleep. Did you have anything else to add?"

"Just a small bit. I think we should all be aware that for a suitor to give his intended the number of gifts of the magnitude present in this song implies his social and economic status. This male has enough money to not only purchase gold, but also other humans, to give to his love. Human culture has huge inequities in it that are still present to this day. Much of this is caused by their addictive love of possessions. That is all," said Bu.

"I don't think there's anyone in this room who would disagree with you," said Lula. "We humans are a young species. We're still struggling and evolving as a culture. There are individuals who still hoard money, possessions and power, but they are slowly being removed from all that. Such huge change takes time, but I have hope that they will finally occur in my lifetime. The Unity has been a great help with that," said Lula. "Is anyone having problems pulling together their presentation?"

The room was silent.

"I think we're done then. Thank you Kleep for an enlightening evening."

Ci had Kleep bow.

Kleep smiled inwardly. Everything had gone perfectly. There was even no need now to return the rings. The man in gray had done his job perfectly, alerting the police. The diplomatic immunity would cover him as well.

SIX GEESE A-LAYING

Renata/Jolie stood at the sink trying to get her long white chocolate-colored hair untangled. She usually brushed it at night and put her hair up, but last night after the Embassy party the ordeal had been too much.

Why could she not be grateful for what she had? Always having to push, push and push some more. Trying to advance her career and get to the next level up.

Jolie/Renata waited patiently for her other head to finish grooming. She'd chosen short chocolate-colored hair for a reason. Simply wet it down in the morning, run her fingers through it and done.

A tentacle reached up to pat down a wayward clump of spiky hair.

"What are we doing for the presentation tonight, again?" asked Renata/Jolie.

"Goose egg."

"Why not geese? Everyone would like to see geese. Remember what a hit those hens were?"

"Do you really want to spend your clothing allowance for the month to rent 6 noisy, squawking geese?

"Good point," said Renata/Jolie, twisting her long hair up into an elaborate bun for the day at work. "But a golden goose egg is expensive."

"We'll hang on to it for a while, then resell it. Gold always goes up. If nothing else, we can sell it on Duveilia for a profit, when we visit or return for good. Things from Earth are a novelty there. Always someone willing to pay."

"True."

Then Renata/Jolie put a gold earring in each ear, tasteful earrings this morning. Last night they'd been gaudy.

"They were not gaudy," said Renata/Jolie.

"I wouldn't have worn them," said Jolie/Renata.

"No. Because you're too conservative."

"I've got to be. Someone has to uphold our reputation. Time to go," said Jolie/Renata.

"I haven't even finished my coffee."

"In the car. Traffic is ugly this morning."

Renata/Jolie groaned.

She went to the tiny kitchen and poured her coffee into the large gold travel mug while her two tentacles pulled on a raincoat the precise milky-brown color of the finest Duveilian chocolate.

She grabbed her bag and the coffee mug, then left her spacious apartment. In the parking lot, she got into the Duveilian Embassy auto car parked in her space.

As it drove through the rain to the freeway, Renata/Jolie sipped her coffee. Rich from milk, intense from the coffee beans and a few dissolved chocolate nibs. Perfect.

It was going to be a busy day. The final draft of the contract between the Idatana Chocolate Corporation and the

Duveilian Chocolate Empire needed to be gone over and checked for errors. Then sent on to signatories. All that was Jolie/Renata's work for the day. She needed to be at her peak.

Which left Renata/Jolie in charge of acquiring a golden egg for tonight.

The car let them off at the covered employee entrance to the Embassy. Other upper echelon Embassy staff were also arriving early. There were many other important contracts being negotiated today. Lower level staff would arrive later at another door. Visitors to the Embassy through yet another entrance.

Renata/Jolie took the elevator to her spacious office on the second from the top floor and shed the raincoat, hanging it in the closet and setting the temperature to dry whatever errant drops might have found it.

She sat in her chair, pulled up a screen and began scrolling sources of golden objects with her left hand, while Jolie/Renata pulled up another screen to look at the contract and make corrections with her right hand.

She worked through first coffee break. Missing the expansive view of Puget Sound out the huge windows. The sun peeked out for the only time it would show its face during the day. A peregrine falcon caught a pigeon in full view. Her tentacles massaged stiff shoulder muscles. Still, she worked on.

A few minutes before noon, Derek/Kianan sent through a last minute change of several clauses that she'd already checked for accuracy. Jolie/Renata grumbled, but incorporated them, checking them for errors, sending him a note that any more changes would delay the signing.

At 1 p.m., Renata/Jolie said, "It's time for lunch. Now. I can't wait any longer."

Jolie/Renata sighed, running a hand through her short spiky hair.

"All right. But we've got to eat at the Embassy. Not enough time to go out."

She rose and took the elevator down two floors to the Executive Dining Room. Many Duveilians seemed to be having a late lunch today.

Mariana/Wimini waved at her. Renata/Jolie waved back and went over to share a table.

"Oh, it's good to see you," said Mariana/Wimini.

"It's been too long. What's the special for today?"

"Something called roast goose."

"Yuck. I've had enough of geese."

"Geese, is that the same as goose?"

"Plural. It's a large Earth bird."

"I have to say I don't have a grasp of the local animals."

"It's that study group I'm in. I have to do a presentation tonight."

"But you're in the middle of a huge contract. Surely they understand you've got more important things to do than prepare for a presentation."

"Really, not much preparation needed. But it's about geese. Sort of."

Renata/Jolie ordered her usual. A green salad laden with steak, gorgonzola cheese and walnuts. And more coffee. She'd follow it with a luscious chocolate dessert.

"Well, I'm trying the goose," said Mariana/Wimini.

"I'd like a bite," said Jolie/Renata.

"Traitor," said Renata/Jolie.

"I want to understand what all the humans saw in it."

"So, what's up in Contracts?" asked Wimini/Mariana.

"Last minute changes," said Jolie/Renata. "And there's a

huge celebration party being planned for the weekend. When everything should be wrapped up. Want to come?"

"Do I?" said Wimini/Mariana, laughing.

"I'll let you know the details once I get them."

Wimini/Mariana had made no secret of her interest in Kianan/Derek. He was always too busy to notice her, but she kept trying.

They were all eating when the Ambassador came in, followed by the Travel Minister, Security Minister, Trade Minister, Public Relations Minister and Translation Minister. They sat at their reserved table without acknowledging anyone else, obviously deep in conversation.

"Well, that's unusual. They never come here," said Mariana/Wimini.

"I wonder what's going on?" asked Renata/Jolie.

"Can I have a taste of your goose?" asked Jolie/Renata.

"Certainly. It's good," said Wimina/Mariana.

The meat was good. Rich and moist. Better than chicken or turkey. She'd have to add that to their presentation tonight.

"You should taste it," said Jolie/Renata.

"No. I'll take your word for it," said Renata/Jolie.

After Renata/Jolie had finished the meal, the Ministers were still dining and talking. She would have loved to overhear every word. But that contract was waiting. If she finished it early, she could leave and beat some of the traffic.

There was that presentation and she'd have to arrive on time. The rain and darkness outside ensured traffic would be terrible again. One would think that humans would be intelligent enough to let go of their insistence on driving themselves, but cars seemed somehow imbedded in their psyches as a symbol of independence and freedom. Too many humans wouldn't allow a car to drive for them, no matter how impaired they might be. Every being in a vehicle suffered because of it. Lula was right, change was slow here.

Back in her office, Jolie/Renata applied herself to the contract, moving through it rapidly, finding errors and correcting them. Renata/Jolie planned out their social calendar and wardrobe for the next month.

Jolie/Renata said to the screen, "Send this contract to the signatories." Then she stood up and stretched. It was 4 p.m. Finished an hour early.

"Good, let's go," said Renata/Jolie.

"Have you got the egg?"

"It's been delivered to our building. The staff in the lobby have it."

"Good."

It only took an hour to get home. She collected the package and went up to her apartment on the top floor.

She hadn't opened the shades this morning, but did so now, just in time to see a shaft of sunlight before it sank below the horizon. The days were so short here at this time of year. The city had already begun to light up.

Renata/Jolie had a quick dinner of leftover grilled chicken and salad greens. Then put on a pair of tight black pants and pulled out an equally form-fitting sweater in a mauve color. She threaded her tentacles through their sleeves, followed by her arms and each head. Then pulled the sweater down so it clung to her muscular body in all the right places. Then slipped on warm socks and some cute short black boots. Very retro.

Then the hair brushing commenced.

"Should I wear my hair up?" asked Renata/Jolie.

Jolie/Renata rolled her eyes.

"It's just a presentation for a silly study group. Don't you think that's a little formal?"

"You're right. Down it is."

When Renata/Jolie had finally finished her preparations, she opened the package. Inside was a large red box, covered with fabric. Inside the box was an egg all right, but it wasn't exactly golden. It was decorated in gold colors, along with red and yellow and blue. The decoration was painted on in incredibly intricate and precise patterns. It was absolutely stunning.

"Um, that's not what I ordered," said Renata/Jolie.

"But it is beautiful."

The egg was light and she could see a tiny hole in one end.

"Look, here's a card. *This egg was created using the age-old art of pysanky. The interior of the goose egg was removed from the small hole at one end and the shell hand painted by Irina.*"

Jolie/Renata looked at the egg.

"Well, it's a goose egg. We'll run with it."

She put it back in the red box and latched it closed. Then stuck it inside her bag. Leaving their apartment, they went down to the front door and took the waiting Embassy car to the group.

Despite having given hundreds of presentations Renata/Jolie was nervous. Dinner wasn't sitting well on her stomach. And she worried her preparations weren't enough. She was representing Duveilia to all these other beings. Many of whom had done superb presentations. Some even at great risk to their beings.

And she had what? A goose egg. An empty goose egg. Made into art, but still, an empty goose egg. What if it wasn't enough?

She would have arrived half an hour early. Plenty of time

to relax and chat with the others. If there hadn't been two completely separate accidents on the freeway.

As it was, Renata/Jolie got to the group just on time. Everyone else was already there. Waiting.

"Sorry, I'm late," Renata/Jolie said. "I left early, but there were two accidents tonight."

She shrugged off her raincoat, draping it over an empty chair.

Lula shook her head. "Traffic is terrible. There is legislation moving through the system to ban human-driven vehicles from the road, but I can't see it passing anytime soon. Get yourself ready and we'll begin."

Renata/Jolie took her place at the front of the room, holding the red box in her left tentacle. She remained standing.

"Good evening everyone. I did a lot of research for this song lyric. There wasn't much to unearth. *On the sixth day of Christmas, my true love gave to me six geese a-laying.* One version changed it to ducks. But there you are. Geese. At this time in human history geese were commonly eaten. So were their eggs. A flock of geese was common on most family farms and goose would have been the main course at a Christmas dinner. They fell out of favor when factory farms took over. They weren't suited to being grown en masse, however rich and juicy their meat is. The Embassy lunch room served it today and I tasted it. Very, very good. And by the way, geese don't lay eggs around Christmastime. So whoever wrote the song, really knew little about birds. This is the second bird mistake they made, the first was with the turtle doves migration."

Renata/Jolie paused for a breath.

"So the lover would have been giving his intended a

never-ending supply of goose meat and eggs. But there's also another popular story about geese. A fable about a goose. A man had a goose. One day she laid a golden egg. The next day another. This continued on, making the man quite wealthy. But he wanted more. One golden egg a day wasn't enough for him. So he cut open the goose, trying to find the source of the gold. He found nothing and now the goose was dead and would never lay another egg. Fables have a moral. This one was: don't kill the source of your wealth. I was going to bring a golden egg to show you, one I bought, but serendipity intervened and I was sent this instead," said Renata/Jolie.

She opened the box and took out the painted egg.

There were murmurs from the group.

"This is a goose egg. They're much larger than chicken eggs. As are geese. The egg has been drained of its contents and hand painted by an artist named Irina. I believe it's one of the most beautiful things I've ever seen. It's a testament to patience and skill. The egg is hollow and incredibly fragile, so I'll set it on the table over here so you can all see it more closely, but I ask that you don't touch it. I'm not sure the egg could take handling," said Renata/Jolie.

She walked over to a table and pulled the stand out of the box. It had come with the egg. She set it on the table, placing the egg upon it. The study group members came up to admire it.

"Amazingly fine work," said Magwab.

"I didn't know humans could do such things," said Niida.

"Wondrous," said Squip.

Renata/Jolie was especially grateful she hadn't let Squip handle the egg. Who knows what effect her slime would have had on the egg's paint?

Lula said, "This is a special art form called Ukranian painted eggs. It came from a region on the other side of the planet. Each egg is hand painted and different from any other. Individual artist have their own styles. Painted eggs are handed down through generations. Not many people practice this art any more. This is truly a treasure. Thank you Renata/Jolie. I'm learning so much through this group and I hope all of you are too."

"I sure am," said Daisy.

"Me too," said Vert.

Renata/Jolie beamed with pride and bowed in acknowledgement.

After the meeting, she packaged the egg back up in its red box and set it inside her large bag.

The ride back home was spent in silence. She'd done well. It had been an exhausting day, what with the contract and her presentation.

In her apartment, Renata/Jolie cleared off a small table and spread a gold metallic cloth on it. Then she set up the stand with the egg. Such a treasure, Lula was right. Some other being had spent hours and hours creating it. It was more valuable than any golden egg.

The least Renata/Jolie could do was give it a place of honor and appreciate it fully.

She sat on the couch with a mug of relaxing warm chocolate and admired the egg. She would never have been as foolish as to kill the goose. Not having a goose, she would be grateful for the egg.

Perhaps she didn't need to climb to the next level. Maybe she was fine just where her career had landed her.

She would ponder that for a season or two.

At least through Christmas.

SEVEN SWANS A-SWIMMING

Daisy did one more pull-up. That was it. He was done for the day. Exercise was not pleasant, but a necessity on such a high-gravity planet as Earth. Otherwise his body would be destroyed by the time he left to return to Catalpa.

He walked barefoot through his indoor field of Catalpan plants, into the bathroom, took off the workout clothes and stood in the shower.

His thoughts strayed to Marishka, of the dark eyes and flashing wit. She had left him for another. One who was more adventurous. Leaving him broken and hurting.

Daisy let the tears fall, cleansed by the shower. He needed to get over her. And to get over the pain. To become whole again. The water shut off. It was nearly time to go.

Today he was on loan from the Catalpan Embassy. Working in the Sartalan Embassy. Translating for them as their translator didn't speak Gaelic. The Scots had a bias against English and refused to speak it, which was unfortunate, because that had become the official Unity language for Earth. But the Scots apparently had a long bitter history with

England. So, the Sartalans were indulging them and paying for a translator.

Daisy dressed in loose black pants and a black shirt. The color of invisibility in negotiations. Then pulled the white hair on top of his head into a braid, along with an orange ribbon to signify gender. He didn't wear any other ornamentation, not wanting to be a distraction, although he did shift the color of his skin to a slight gray color with a scaled pattern to it. It was subtle and tasteful.

He sipped a juice of fruit and vegetables. Then stood for a moment, his feet and hands touching the plants in his apartment. Connecting with them and through their juicy green growth, opening himself to the energy of the multiverse.

It filled him with peace and energy for the day.

At the door, Daisy put on heated socks and black boots that were flexible enough for his feet to move efficiently. And a raincoat with a hood. The fall rains had come and they were cold. Catalpans needed warmth.

"Until tonight, my friends," he said, to the plants cohabiting with him.

Before leaving the building, Daisy stood in the small clean room. The inner and outer doors closed, gravity was adjusted to mirror the outside. Daisy's shoes and clothes were cleaned of any possible seeds, pollen or plant-life. Then the outer door opened and Daisy stepped out.

He walked through the parking lot to the Embassy flying car. After programming it with his schedule, Daisy sat back and enjoyed the ride. The car lifted off and joined in the stream of vehicles moving towards the center of the city.

The rain had stopped and Seattle sparkled like a freshly-washed crystal. Even without any direct sunlight.

Daisy pulled up a screen and looked at his schedule. Tomorrow was the study group again. His presentation was due. He'd done plenty of research, but still hadn't come up with a plan. He'd work on it tonight.

He was gaining much from the group. Learning more about the other beings than about humans. That was good, since most of his work was with other Unity members. He wished Magwab had already done his presentation. It would have helped to know more about Sartalans in preparation for today. But he would do fine. He was simply interpreting, not negotiating for either side.

The car landed in front of the Sartalan Embassy and Daisy got out. He entered through the front door. The building was massive, completely carved of rough gray and red stone. There had to be places where the blocks joined together, but they were hidden by the texture.

Inside, the overwhelming smell of peanut butter permeated the Embassy. So it wasn't just Magwab. All Sartalans smelled like that.

Several guards, wearing only weapons and the fur they were born with, patrolled the lobby as if the Embassy was on alert. Was something wrong or was this normal?

The lobby was large, making the Sartalans present and the few visitors seem insignificant.

He closed his eyes and did his best to sense around him. There were no plants to help. The guards were laughing quietly about something. They seemed at ease. Perhaps this many armed guards was normal.

Daisy walked up to the front desk made of gray stone and presented his ID.

"I'm here to interpret. Room 448."

"I'll have a guard take you up there," said the Sartalan standing behind the desk.

Daisy nodded and waited. The lobby was cold, not just the energy, but the temperature. He might leave the raincoat on all day.

As he watched the guards, Daisy began to notice the differences in color and patterns in their fur.

A guard came up and said, "I'll take you to the conference room."

Daisy nodded and followed the guard to an elevator, which he recognized as Catalpan tech. It felt odd to see organic tech in this cold fortress of stone. Still rocks were organic too. Their life processes were simply so much slower than other living beings, they went along unnoticed.

"Daisy, is that you?" asked the guard, once they were moving upwards.

"Magwab? I didn't recognize you."

"All of us Sartalans look alike, right?" Magwab grinned, his sharp teeth obvious.

"No, you don't. But you were the first Sartalan I've ever seen. Until I came here, I didn't realize that you're all different."

"The various patterns and colors are clan and class markings."

"So, you are born at one level and stay there your entire life?"

"Not exactly. There's fluidity among the classes. You're stuck with your clan though. Family is always there."

Daisy nodded.

"Are that many armed guards in the lobby normal?"

"We have more than some embassies. We are always under threat."

"I don't know enough about Sartalans."

"But you're negotiating."

"No, I'm merely interpreting. I'm not a negotiator."

"How's your presentation coming," asked Magwab. "You're up tomorrow, right?"

"I am. I'll come up with something."

"I couldn't do that. I've been working on mine for weeks, but not getting anywhere. I hope it'll be good enough."

"I just can't think of anything new. There are entirely too many birds in that song."

Magwab laughed, a deep menacing sound.

"I just want to eat them. You don't eat meat, do you? Sorry."

"I eat meat. Probably not as much as Sartalans. Catalpans have a plant-based diet, but we are omnivores."

Magwab nodded. The elevator stopped and they got out. Then walked down the corridor, which looked like an underground tunnel.

They stopped at a room. The doorway was rounded at the top, as if carved out of the stone, and a sign on the metal door read 448.

Magwab opened the door and the lights switched on in the windowless room. The lights were on the reddish side of the spectrum and gave the cold gray stone a warm feeling. Fur-covered cushions sitting on the floor. No one else was present.

"Looks like you're the first one here."

"That was my plan. It's always best for the interpreter to arrive first and not leave the two negotiating sides unable to speak with each other."

"I hadn't thought of that," said Magwab. "Good idea. Well, see ya tomorrow night."

"It was interesting seeing you at work," said Daisy.

Magwab left the door open and disappeared back into the elevator.

Daisy took a cushion for himself and put it at one end of the floor. Then he divided the rest of the cushions in two piles, arranging them in a line across from each other. He hoped nine cushions was enough. It was always helpful if negotiating teams brought the same number of beings.

The floor seemed to be heated. Which felt good after the coolness of the lobby.

The Scots arrived next. There were four of them, evenly divided between male and female. The two men wore kilts and the two women, long pants. All of them wore heavy sweaters and no protection from the rain.

"Good morning," said Daisy, in Gaelic.

"Good morning," said the bearded man, looking relieved at Daisy's Gaelic. He shook Daisy's extended hand.

"I'm Daisy. I'll be your interpreter today."

"Daisy. That's a peculiar name for someone not from Earth."

"We Catalpans often take names from Earth to make it easier for humans. Our birth names are unpronounceable by humans. Your vocal system is arranged differently than ours."

The bearded man nodded.

"I'm Ian, this is Glenn, Aisla and Gara."

"We're still awaiting the Sartalan negotiators, but have a seat if you'd like."

Ian looked at the pillows on the floor and raised his eyebrows.

"Is this how Sartalans normally do business?"

"I know very little about Sartalans. I did learn that their

differing fur patterns are clan and class markings. I believe your people also divide themselves up into clans."

"Aye, we do," said Ian.

The Sartalans arrived. There were four of them as well, although Daisy couldn't tell their gender aside from the gender markers.

Daisy introduced himself again.

The Sartalans didn't shake hands, but nodded respectfully as he introduced the Scots. A fifth Sartalan brought a floating tray into the room.

Everyone arrayed themselves on the pillows and the fifth Sartalan, who was never introduced, served all of them mugs of hot kilan. It tasted like a cross between hot coffee, chocolate and black tea. Daisy decided he liked it very much.

The negotiations began after minimal pleasantries were exchanged. Each side praising the reputation of the others'. They were negotiating a biotech agreement. Scotland was on the cutting edge of biotech, with only minimal assistance from the Unity.

The Sartalans needed a great deal of help in that area. They were brilliant at warfare and, surprisingly, peacemaking. Their skills lay in interpersonal interactions rather than science.

Daisy did his job, watching how the two parties countered each other's offers. Only once did things become heated. Daisy did what he could to use non-inflammatory language while interpreting their words. And made every attempt to be fair to each side.

Finally, a deal was struck. The final language of the contract hammered out and recorded on tablets, with Daisy making sure each side's contract in their own native language was the same as the other's.

There had been only one break. For lunch, they'd been served in the same room. The food was rich, meaty and spicy. Followed by a cooling fruit drink of some sort.

They spent the entire day sitting, except for bathroom breaks. Daisy didn't mind, but the Scots kept getting up to stretch their legs. Having joints was not something he envied. Although being able to live comfortably in such high-gravity as Earth, was wearing on him.

The day finally ended at 8 p.m. Long after Daisy's dinner. But everything had been accomplished. The deal was done and everyone seemed pleased with the result.

The Sartalan's walked everyone down to the lobby. Daisy had called his car and walked through the rain to it. The Scots walked through the rain like it was nothing. Their van waited too.

Traffic was thick, so Daisy stopped at a drive-through and ordered hot vegetable soup. It was the perfect choice. He tasted sweet carrots, onions, oregano and tomatoes. There were mustard greens, mushrooms and green peas floating in it.

By the time Daisy got home, he was ready for bed. The presentation would have to wait for tomorrow. He was too exhausted now.

The next day, Daisy went into the Embassy to write a report about the previous day. He entered into the clean room. Then in the secondary entrance, as was customary, he removed his shoes and placed them in a box to retrieve upon exiting.

Daisy walked through the lobby, his feet reveling in the texture of the soft grasslike plants growing there. He connected with the plant's energy and felt their welcome. A feeling of well-being filled him.

As he continued through the lobby, the change in gravity became noticeable. The building was sealed and Catalpan gravity simulated. It felt so freeing.

He bounced up the ramp to the second floor. The floor to ceiling windows let in as much light as they could. It wasn't enough, so warm light flowed down from the ceiling and through skylights. Every surface was covered with plants. Even the building itself was a living, breathing entity. More plant than tech.

Daisy went to sit in one of the private offices on a living bench. This room, too, was filled with happily growing plants. They filtered the air, adding their own scents. The energy they gave off exuded a vitality which made other environments feel dead.

Because of their connection to plants, as necessary as breathing, the Catalpans had been allowed to bring most of their native plants to Earth. So long as they kept them within their own enclosed environments and had clean rooms on every exit. It was a small price to pay for that relationship.

As he spoke to the screen, one of the interns brought a long brown paper box to him.

Daisy opened it and inside found a large bunch of white daisies, their stems in plastigel to keep them fresh. A message arrived on his screen at the same moment.

We wanted to thank you for your graciousness yesterday. The beauty and purity of your words are reflected in these daisies. Which also symbolize love, purity and beauty. May the road rise up to meet you. May the wind be always at your back. May the sun shine warm upon your face; the rains fall soft upon your fields until we meet again.

It was from the Scots.

Daisy smiled as things clicked together in his mind. Catalpans didn't normally smile, but Daisy had picked up the habit from interacting with so many beings who did.

After writing the report, he set up his schedule for the next few weeks. Then attended a meeting for translators. The rest of the afternoon, he spent learning more Lushootseed from watching old vids of tribal elders telling stories and teaching young children the language.

He decided not to go home before the study group. That would just add more time to sit in traffic. Instead, Daisy showered at the Embassy and dressed in fresh warm clothing. He ordered a meal from one of the Embassy restaurants and while waiting, spent the time in one of the meditation rooms.

The room felt warm and was filled with the plants from Daisy's youth. It glowed with warm light. By the time he left the room, Daisy felt calm and refreshed. Ready for his presentation.

The dinner was a salad of greens picked from the Embassy's vast indoor gardens. There were other vegetables, fruits and nutmeats added as well. Good food that nurtured his body and energetic system.

The drive to the study group was in the dark and wet. The lights from vehicles and streetlights glinted across the car windows, streaked by the rain. At least it was warm in the car. Daisy played the sound of a melodic brook.

Traffic was surprisingly light. It only took an hour to arrive at the meeting place. So Daisy was half an hour early. He carried the plastigel with his daisies into the building.

The lights were on in the meeting room, but no one else was there. Daisy rearranged the chairs. Someone had used the room since the last study group and left the chairs lined up against the walls.

Daisy rearranged them so the audience faced the large

windows and looked out into the darkness beyond. Satisfied, he sat on his chair looking towards the audience. The daisies sat on the floor in front of him.

The dead, human building felt cold, but he could deal with it for a short time. He'd worn warmer clothes for this evening. He folded his legs up onto the chair, sitting on them. Then closed his eyes, meditating and waiting for the others.

Martha was the first to arrive, followed by Niida. One by one the rest of them arrived. Lula arrived last, as seemed her custom.

"Good evening everyone," said Lula. "Daisy, are you ready?"

"I am," he said. "Welcome everyone. I invite you to relax and lean back in your chairs. Leave the cares of your day behind. My presentation is on Day 7. *On the seventh day of Christmas, my true love gave to me seven swans a-swimming.* Now swans are very special beings. They have a long history in Earth's various mythologies. A swan is symbolic of grace, beauty, purity and love. They are very beautiful birds who mate for life. The swans our lover would have been gifting would be mute swans, native to Europe and Asia. They are large graceful birds. Their wingspan is as wide as I am tall. They're referred to in myth, fairy tales, literature and ballet. At the time this song was written, all swans in England were considered to belong to the Crown. And those who purchased a right to own swans, from the Crown. So our lover was very wealthy if they were able to own swans in order to gift them. I'm not sure if he actually purchased a swan mark for her, as it was called. So *she* didn't actually own the swans, unless her family owned a swan mark. But as was the human custom back then, the woman was *owned* by her father and would become the lover's property when they married. Human traditions have not always been as enlightened as they are now. The swans and all the woman's other belongings were actually the property of whoever owned her. Anything her lover gave her, would actually become his if she married him. Quite a self-serving gift.

"Swans were also eaten, by the very wealthy, and often for Christmas dinner. So our lover was again reinforcing his suitability as a suitor by displaying his wealth and gifting his intended with food. Beyond that he was appreciating her beauty and grace. And acknowledging her purity while acclaiming his love. In one masterful gift. That's a lot rolled into one grand gesture.

"I have no swans here tonight. They are larger even than geese and mute swans are highly regulated in this country, as they are not native. I have a different symbol of love, grace and purity. I was gifted these today," said Daisy, picking up the vase. "I didn't even realize the flower I took for my name also symbolized the same qualities. I'll pass them around and you may each take one home with you. As you do that, I'll pass along the blessing that came with them.

"*May the road rise up to meet you. May the wind be always at your back. May the sun shine warm upon your face; the rains fall soft upon your fields until we meet again,*" said Daisy.

The daisies got passed around the room, each class participant taking a flower. Magwab sniffed at it and nodded to Daisy, smiling.

Asoona took the flower and inserted it into the shiny jeweled pin on his shirt. Renata/Jolie tucked it in her hair.

Lula was the last to take one.

She said, "Thank you Daisy. I'm so pleased with all of your presentations. You are a very inventive group. If no one has any questions, I'll see you next time. We have five more presentations to go."

No one had any questions. They left the room, quietly, as if in meditation.

Daisy felt full. Whole. He hadn't felt this way in a very, very long time. Since before Marishka. He was healing. Perhaps even healed. Ready to move forward with his life.

There was one daisy left. He brought it with him to the car. He might even be able to make it grow with the right nutrients to stimulate roots and leaves. It would be interesting to see how Earth plants mingled with Catalpan ones. What sort of energy would Earth plants exude?

He liked his life here on Earth. Even with the heavy gravity.

It was time to begin enjoying it again.

EIGHT MAIDS A-MILKING

Asoona gazed out over the vast Tolpian Embassy lobby. No one had come in at all today, except employees. No one had needed his help. He felt useless.

He wanted to help someone. Anyone. With anything.

How could he fulfill his mission in life if there was no one to help?

He'd watched the clouds move across the sky above the great transparent dome of the embassy. Once or twice the sun had even come out, heating the lobby almost to the point of comfort. Almost.

Tolpians adored the heat. The other rooms in the embassy were fiery warm, but the lobby with its tall glass doors let heat out and cold in whenever the other embassy workers went in or out. Which was every 7.4 minutes. He'd timed it.

Just as the heat in the lobby began to build, the doors opened again. There was supposed to be a remodel done to fix the problem, but it hadn't been scheduled yet.

Asoona wore a purple cardigan, hot pink fingerless gloves

and a blue wool hat that tied beneath his snout. One of the humans who often came to the embassy made it for him. She'd seen him shivering and knew that human hats wouldn't fit a reptilian head. And Tolpians didn't wear hats on their planet because it was warm enough. Blue was currently his favorite color. She'd made the strings that tied it orange, so he'd have his gender identifier. So very thoughtful.

A small portable heater blazed behind the desk, but it only heated his lower body. Asoona kept moving the heater from side to side, in order to keep both sides of him warm.

He felt bored. He should be working on his presentation. But he'd hit a roadblock. How did one find eight maids a-milking? In an era when machines did all the milking.

He'd contacted every dairy within a hundred miles. Not that there were many in this region. Two of the listings had gone out of business. A third one retired. The area around New Seattle wasn't rural anymore.

Asoona searched for any other possible meaning of the song lyric. Some versions used Ladies Dancing. Others hounds or hares a-running. Another had boys singing. But most of the versions were maids a-milking. Asoona wanted to make his presentation true to the song.

He was running out of time. He'd procrastinated for far too long. The day after tomorrow was the day. So far he had nothing.

Putting his head down on the desk, Asoona covered his eyes with gloved hands. He simply wanted to disappear. This study group wasn't worth it. It only caused stress in his life. He didn't need any more stress. Here he was in midlife. With no partners. No female and no neuter. His life was loveless and he was alone. An awful thing for a Tolpian.

Tolpians lived for love. Their entire days, weeks and years

filled with finding new ways to express love. For themselves, each other and the entire multiverse.

Asoona had been looking for love and not finding it. Tolpians here on Earth were different than on Tolpia. They were all so busy. And he wasn't. The study group was his only extra thing. Others went to fashion shows, out dancing and to a continual stream of social events.

Asoona hadn't been here long enough to get invited out. And he was one of the lowest level Embassy employees. Tolpians did pay attention to rank.

He moaned as the doors shooshed open again. Grudgingly, he looked up.

"Martina," he said, to the human with wrinkly eyes.

"Good afternoon, Asoona. Well, that hat fits you perfectly. How are the gloves?"

"They're good, but I'm still cold."

"You need a long coat then. I'm cold too. This fall's been crispy and winter's right around the corner."

"I can't even imagine what winter will be like. Will I ever be warm again?"

"You will. Spring and summer will come again. How's your presentation coming?" asked Martina.

She'd taken off her gloves and leaned on the desk. Her long fingers were wrinkled too. Asoona wasn't sure why. Most humans had enhancements to change personal defects.

"Terribly."

He explained the problem to her.

"Well, your lyric just says *maids a-milking*, right? They don't have to be milking cows."

"Isn't that where milk comes from?"

"All mammals have milk for their young, even humans. We've mostly used cows' milk. I know some cultures milked mares. But our culture has also used goats' milk. A friend of mine owns goats and makes fancy cheeses from their milk."

"Goats. Does your friend live nearby?"

"About an hour away. If there's no traffic. Should I arrange for you to visit?"

"My presentation is on Thursday."

"How about tomorrow? Are you working here?"

"I am owed days off. I could see about taking one tomorrow."

"Good. I'll call her and see if we can come."

"You'd come with me?" he asked.

"Yes. It's been a while since I've seen her and it's always good to visit old friends. Even better to introduce them to new friends."

Asoona's heart warmed. Martina considered him a friend. It had been so long since he'd had a friend.

"I'll go up to my meeting and check back in with you before I leave," she said.

"That's good. I'll see about scheduling the day off."

By the time she returned, Asoona had spoken with his supervisor and had the day off.

"Oh good," said Martina. "Where should I pick you up?"

"I live at the Tolpian Palisades."

"I know where that is. I'll be there at 9 a.m."

"Perfect," he said.

"Why is it called a palisade? That's a type of fence in French."

"The developers thought it sounded like palace. They apparently didn't look it up."

She laughed and he did too.

"Everyone wants to be grander than they really are. I'll see you tomorrow. And dress warmly, we'll be outside."

"I will certainly do that. I've grown weary of being cold. But this will be a great adventure."

"That it will, my friend."

After work, he went shopping. Not to the fashion stores, but to the outdoors stores.

Asoona was difficult to fit, but the staff kindly helped him find a long coat with sleeves he could roll up. He also bought some stretchy green pants that would fit his short legs, if he cut them off. And he bought two sets of something called gaiters to put on his tail to keep it warm and dry if it was raining. And a soft warm scarf topped off the purchases.

The next morning Asoona dressed in his new finery, cutting the pants to fit. He wore warm socks and shoes, even though shoes always felt uncomfortable. He'd need the warmth and it was raining out already.

Before 9 a.m., Asoona had eaten a full breakfast of fresh fruits and greens, was fully outfitted and downstairs in the warm lobby of Tolpian Palisades. This large glass lobby was at least well insulated. There were separate in and and out doors. Each contained two chambers to the entrance and the inner one wouldn't open until all the cold air had been sucked out and replaced with warmth. It took longer to get in and out of the building, but wasted less energy to heat it.

Martina arrived just on time in a bright red car. It was small, of the type humans called sports cars.

Asoona left the building and walked out into the cold, glad for the warmth of his new clothes. He held his tail curled up, so the gaiters wouldn't drag on the ground.

Getting in the small car, Asoona realized Martina was actually driving. He'd never been in a car that was driven by a person.

"Good morning, hop in and I'll crank the heat up."

Asoona awkwardly sat down in the seat, trying to find a place for his tail and finally ended up sitting on it. The seat restraints came on as he closed the door, strapping him in.

"I didn't know you drove."

"I never drive in the city, too much traffic. But we're going out to the sticks. The autocars don't work as well out there. They're not programmed for the kind of obstacles we might meet. And I like to take this baby out for a spin now and then."

Asoona nodded, feeling more than a little nervous.

"It looks like you went shopping last night," Martina said, pulling out onto the road.

"I did. I found all sorts of warm clothes."

"Good. I sure hope your embassy fixes the heat problem in the lobby soon."

"So do I."

They got on the freeway leading away from town. Traffic in that direction was light. Martina sped along in the fast lane without a problem.

"How long have you been friends with this person who owns goats?"

"Since we went to college. We both majored in art. Cass went on to live in the country and paint. She's world-famous now. The goats were pets and the dairy farm and cheese making came about a result of having them."

"You are world-famous as well," said Asoona.

"Yes, I am, I suppose. That's why I'm creating the murals to be hung in your embassy. Only I crochet in my spare time, not raise goats. It's much simpler." She laughed.

Asoona joined in with her laughing.

"What about you? What did you specialize in at school?"

"Like all Tolpians, I specialized in love. Although I haven't found my female and my neuter yet."

"Is that what you call your mates?"

"Yes. Not just mates though, soul mates."

"Don't Tolpians usually find them early in life?"

"Yes. Although some have found them on their deathbeds. Yet, I grow weary of being alone."

"I can understand that. You Tolpians seem to live for love in a way even us romantic humans don't. Oh, some humans live for love, but I'm not one of them. I've had flings, but never found anyone I wanted to spend my life with. And now, I care less than ever before."

"Why?"

She glanced at him sideways.

"I'm old. Nearly ninety. I may have ten or so years left before I die. Maybe more, maybe less. I have friends and family. I don't really need a life partner."

Asoona felt appalled. He hadn't known she was that old. Humans lived such short lives.

"Shocked you, didn't I? I know I don't look that old. But I am. There's so many enhancements these days. I haven't gotten rid of wrinkles or permanently colored my hair. I used my credits to buy stronger bones, better eyesight. And other things to keep my body running well. So I don't look feeble or move like someone who's ancient. If I don't have my body and eyes, I don't have my art."

"There is so much I don't understand about humans. That's why I joined this study group. So far it's teaching me more about other beings than humans."

"Knowledge is power. And who knows, perhaps your knowledge about other beings will come in handy. When you become a Tolpian Embassy bigwig, you might need to throw a dinner for Cassion diplomats and you'll at least have a place to begin."

"I think it's unlikely I'll rise far in the Embassy without soul mates."

"Really? Is that how it works?" she asked.

"Most of the time. There are exceptions. For exceptional Tolpians. I am ordinary."

"You are anything but ordinary, my friend. I have befriended none of the others. You are special. Kinder than the others and much more helpful. Which is why I'm helping you."

"Thank you so much for your kindness. I truly appreciate it. I was completely lost about how to do this presentation."

"You're welcome. Thank you for befriending an old woman."

Eventually, they turned off the freeway to smaller and narrower roads. From four lanes to two lanes. Then finally, down a one lane gravel road. The ride became surprisingly bumpy.

The scenery had changed from tall buildings crowding the freeway to large clumps of trees interspersed by green meadows. Some of them had animals grazing. Horses or cows. Asoona couldn't be sure what they were.

The area around Martina's friend's house was filled with tall trees. Taller than many buildings. Asoona hadn't known the area hosted such magnificent trees. He'd never been out of the city, here on Earth.

Tolpia didn't have tall trees. Water wasn't as abundant there as it was here. Trees on his native planet were short and gnarled.

Martina turned off the main gravel road at a wooden sign that read *Lawson's Dairy* and drove up to a small building painted green. It was surrounded on three sides by tall green trees.

There were four other buildings, some smaller, some larger. A human came out of one of them. She limped slightly and had sun-darkened skin, unlike Martina's paler skin. The stranger had even more wrinkles than Martina and long white hair tied back. She wore a shirt that left her arms bare. Even in this cold. It made Asoona shiver.

Martina had turned the engine off and was getting out. Asoona got out and walked around the car to meet her friend.

"Martina! It's so good to see you."

"Cass, this is Asoona. Asoona, my good friend, Cass."

"I'm pleased to meet you," said Asoona, holding out his gloved hand.

Cass shook it with her bare hand.

"Nice to meet you. Martina told me you're interested in seeing the farm. Let me give you a tour and then we can go inside for some hot kilan."

"Can I use your bathroom while Asoona tells you what he needs?" asked Martina.

"Of course, you remember where it is?"

"Yes."

Asoona explained his presentation. A small furry being that was a light orange color with darker stripes, had come out of one of the buildings and was rubbing up against Cass' legs.

"Who is that?" he asked.

Cass bent over and stroked the being, then picked it up.

"This is Mabel. She's the most affectionate cat I've ever owned. Follows me everywhere."

"Cat. I don't think I know about cats."

"She lives here, hunts for mice and rats. Her brother lives here too, he's black. You probably won't see him. He's shy around strangers. You can pet her."

Asoona stoked the cat along her back. Mabel began to rumble.

"She likes you. Listen to her purr."

"What a pleasant sound."

"Yes, it is. Oh, Martina's back. I'll take you both into the milking barn first. I've left one of the gals tied up inside. So you could watch me milking her."

The milking barn seemed to be all made of metal. It shone with cleanliness and smelled like strong herbs. He recognized lavender, but there were other scents as well.

In one corner stood a goat. She had white and brown fur and long floppy ears. The goat came up to Asoona's waist. She made a a plaintive noise when they came into the barn.

Asoona had brought along a recorder so he could document the visit for the presentation. He turned it on and began recording.

"I know Samantha. You want to get milked and go outside with everybody else," said Cass. "Normally, I milk them about 6:30 in the morning. Then turn them out so they can eat."

She went to a large sink and washed her hands with soap and water. Then dried them on a towel hanging on a hook. She picked up a green bucket and a small wooden stool.

The goat was tied by a blue strap around her neck and her midsection. These connected to two other straps hooked to the wall.

Cass set the stool down beside Samantha's back end and plunked down on it. She put the bucket in front of the goats hind legs.

"Here you can see how swollen her teats are. She's filled with milk, even though it's nearly time for milking season to end. She's an older gal. I won't breed her again. She's earned her retirement."

"How long do they have milk, after their babies are born?" asked Martina.

The cat wove around Martina's legs. She picked her up and Mabel began purring again, while watching Cass intently.

"For about ten months. Then I let them rest up. They need to put their energy into making the next batch of young ones."

Cass had grabbed what she'd called teats and was stroking them, releasing the milk into the bucket. Each stroke was punctuated with a squirting sound. It didn't take long for the level in the bucket to get higher.

Cass had her head against the goat's body. The goat had immediately quieted when Cass began milking her and now looked relaxed.

"Good girl," said Cass, pulling the bucket out from beneath the goat. She stood and shoved the stool away with her foot.

"Now I'll take the milk and add it to the rest that I got this morning. It'll be refrigerated. Most of today's batch will be picked up within the hour. I'm part of a cooperative that sells goat milk to stores. So it'll be taken to the co-op's main processing building. They'll pasteurize and bottle it. Then rush it to the stores to sell."

Cass poured the bucket into a metal container. Then took the bucket to the sink and washed it and set it on a rack to dry.

"Are you still making cheese?"

"Yes. I've made all the cheese I'm going to for the year, it's aging. I'll take you over there next."

Cass showed them the milking parlor, where the goats were milked with machines.

"I've got eight stalls. I used to have sixteen goats, so I milked one shift, then the next. I've cut back to eight now. That's enough critters to care for."

"I don't know how you do it," said Martina. "And all by yourself."

"I hire jobs out now and then. But mostly, it's all me. I love it, so I'm not ready to retire. Let's take Samantha out to the herd."

She opened a small refrigerator and pulled out a bright orange carrot. Which she washed, broke into several pieces and gave each one to Samantha. Who ate them eagerly.

"Thank you dear," said Cass, affectionately patting the goat on her side.

She unclipped the long straps tying the goat to the walls. Then led the goat out of the barn. The orange cat bounded behind them. Martina and Asoona followed.

Cass led the goat to a meadow where the others grazed. The goats all looked different. Three were solid black, brown and white. The others had multiple colors, but different markings.

When Samantha arrived, the goats all began talking to each other. Cass removed the straps from Samantha and she ran over to the others.

"This is my current herd."

"What do you do with the babies?" asked Martina.

"I sell them. They're high quality and I've taken care to choose bloodlines that aren't local. So that people around here who are adding to their herds want my kids."

"Baby goats are called kids," said Martina to Asoona.

They toured the industrial kitchen where cheese was made. It too was made mostly of metal. There were two long steel tables.

Cass showed them the coolers where the cheese was aging. She opened the door. It was large enough to walk inside, although the temperature made Asoona shiver. Shelves filled with cheese.

"That's a lot of cheese," said Martina.

"I make most of my income from the cheese. Not that many people are making handmade cheese these days. The milk and kid sales are just a small part of my business."

She walked them through the process of making the cheese.

"I use the milk from my goats and some of the herbs from the garden. I grow a lot of rosemary and lavender. Other things like black pepper and caraway seeds I buy. I've got some cheese in the house for us to taste, if you'd like."

"I'd love to," said Martina.

"I've never tasted goat cheese," said Asoona. "That would be wonderful.

They left the cheese factory and went inside the house. Where thankfully, it was warm.

Cass asked, "Do both of you want kilan?"

"I've never had kilan," said Martina.

"It's from Sartala. Sort of like coffee, tea and hot chocolate mixed together. It's the big thing with all the foodies right now."

"It sounds divine," said Martina. "Asoona, do you want some?"

"Yes. I quite like kilan."

Martina and Asoona sat at a round wooden table in the

kitchen. Unlike the cheese-making building, this one was painted in the rich colors of terra cotta and yellow ochre. It felt warmer than the steel interior of the cheese-kitchen. A large fabric covered part of the brown tile floor. Paintings of trees and streams hung on the wall.

From the refrigerator, Cass pulled out three chunks of cheese. She unwrapped each one and set it on a small wooden board. Then got out crackers and knives and put everything on the round table.

Cass sat down and explained the cheeses.

"This one is a soft cheese. I marinated it with basil, oregano, garlic, black pepper and olive oil. And this one has jalapeño chilis in it. The last one is lavender and lemon."

The kilan was hot and strong. Asoona could almost feel it warming him from the inside out.

The various goat cheeses were very interesting to taste. He hadn't had goat cheese before, but he also hadn't tasted many of the other flavorings before either. So he couldn't be sure which were which. He liked them all.

As they were leaving, Cass gave him a wheel of rosemary goat cheese. Martina got a lemon and lavender.

"You'll need to cut it for your presentation. I hope your group likes it."

"Thank you so very much," said Asoona. "I have enjoyed our time together. It has been so wonderful to see this part of Earth."

He shook her hand again.

"I've enjoyed meeting you. I don't meet many humans, let alone off-worlders."

"If you're ever in New Seattle, come to the Tolpian Embassy. I'd be honored to give you a tour."

"I just might do that," said Cass. "Sometimes I like to get out of the woods."

The trip back to town seemed much shorter than the drive out. Asoona felt calm and relaxed. Martina was a good driver and it had been a wonderful day.

The next day at the Embassy was busy. Outside it was pouring down rain and people needed help. Asoona was pleased he had the foresight to prepare his presentation last night. There had been no time to work on it today.

He grabbed a takeout meal and ate in the autocar on the way to the presentation, leaving two hours early. Just in case.

That was a good idea. Traffic was indeed getting worse, just as Lula had predicted. The heavy rain and extra vehicles on the road caused many accidents.

He arrived ten minutes early. In plenty of time. Niida, Martha and Daisy were already there.

Asoona had dressed for the performance wearing a red cardigan, a transparent green scarf fixed in place with a red and green rhinestone poinsettia pin and a red knitted hat Martina made him.

"Good evening," he said, and went to sit in the speaker's position.

Soon the room filled with the others. Lula and Kleep were the last ones to arrive, barely on time. Kleep hurried to their seat, so as not to be a second late.

"Hello everyone. Well, traffic just keeps getting worse. It took me three hours to get here tonight. A lot of people out shopping and celebrating. Shall we begin?" asked Lula.

Asoona stood and said, "Good evening. My verse is *On the eighth day of Christmas, my true love gave to me eight maids a-milking.* The song has had several variations throughout the years: ladies dancing, hounds or hares a-running, boys a-singing. But mostly it's been maids a-milking. Now most milk humans use comes from cows. And today they're milked by machines, not people. There aren't any dairy farms nearby these days. The closest ones are several hours away. But humans also drink goat milk. A friend of mine knows someone who raises goats, milks them by machine and makes cheese from some of their milk. She took me there yesterday and I have a vid to show you. Cass normally uses milking machines, but milked a goat for us the old-fashioned way so we could see what it entails. I'll project it here in the center of the room if someone would dim the lights."

The lights dimmed and Asoona switched on the vid from his recorder. In the center of the room stood Cass, washing her hands and talking. Then sitting down on the stood and milking the goat. Before she finished, Asoona paused the recorder.

"You can all come over and touch the goat if you wish."

His group-mates stood and entered the center, touching the goat or just looking more closely.

"Ooh, her fur is really rough," said Renata/Jolie.

"Yes, goat fur is," said Asoona. "But in the next few seconds you'll see the cat that Martina is holding. She's very soft. Pet the cat and listen to her purring."

He advanced the vid until Martina and the cat were in it. Everyone petted the cat.

"She's rumbling," said Schoos.

"It's called purring. Cats do that when happy."

He showed them the rest of the vid with the milking parlor and the cheese factory. And then eating the cheese in Cass' kitchen.

"And now I have a treat for you. Cass gave me some rosemary goat cheese. I brought it to share with my friends."

Asoona unwrapped the cheese and set it on a table at one side of the room. He'd sliced it into pieces at home. The group took pieces and began eating it.

"What is rosemary?"

Asoona looked at Lula.

It's an herb," she said. "A plant grown for its flavor or medicinal properties. Or both."

"I love it," said Daisy.

"It's very good," Magwab.

"I've never tasted hard goat cheese like this. Very tasty," said Lula.

"Cass had soft goat cheeses too."

"Well, thank you Asoona. Another wonderful presentation. I'm learning a lot and I hope all of you are too," said Lula.

"I never knew trees grew so large," said Vert.

"Me neither," said Asoona.

Everyone stayed around after his presentation ended and ate cheese and talked. Several of them complimented him on his presentation. It made Asoona feel good about what he'd done.

He rode home in the autocar, rain still pouring down. But he no longer felt lonely.

Instead he felt full and complete. Even if he never found a female and neuter. He'd be fine. He had friends.

NINE LADIES DANCING

Squip rode the bus north to the Lake District of New Seattle. Back home after a busy day at the Setagean Embassy. It was dark outside the rain-streaked windows, but the inside of the bus was dimly lit.

She watched Earthlings, and a few off-worlders, reading. Some even had paper books. Others crocheted or did handwork. Many used tablets. A few dozed.

Dozed, that was a new word for her. She liked the way it sounded.

Squip shifted in her seat. It wasn't comfortable. Her feet didn't even touch the floor, but she loved to ride the bus. It gave her such an opportunity to learn more about Earthlings.

The bus smelled like wet dog. One of the Earthlings had brought their black-haired dog with them. The dog wore a green vest with white print that read *Service Dog*.

Sometimes on the bus she even got to sit near someone who wanted to talk. Not tonight. No one sat near her. This bus was only half full and Earthlings seemed to naturally spread out onto the empty seats rather than all sit together.

Setageans would have clumped together and made a party of the daily trip.

Squip had spent weeks watching the other presentations for the study group. And had no ideas about what to do for her own. Hers was coming up fast. She needed to find something, anything, to do.

Squip had talked about it last night with her podlet, Clarence. She told him about her research.

Her research showed that the last four verses of the song had been exchanged with each other throughout the years. Some versions having ladies dancing on the ninth, tenth, eleventh or twelfth days. With the other last four verses rotating as well. In addition she found the ninth day had also used the gifts of: lambs a-bleating, bulls a-roaring and bears a-beating.

Squip had quickly decided she didn't want to have anything to do with wild beings larger than she was. And as for lambs a-bleating, some quick research told her that most sheep births took place during mid-late winter. Not early December, which was still fall. No lambs for her.

With the two bird errors and one animal error, Squip decided the Earthling who wrote the song didn't really know much about other creatures.

She researched ladies and found that it had been a common name for females as well as a title in certain countries for nobility. Earthlings didn't historically possess other nobles, so Squip decided the verse applied to females.

Now dancing, that was complicated. There were so many types of Earthling dances, she didn't know where to begin.

The bus slowed as her stop came up. Squip slid off the seat and joined the line to get out. She was grateful for the self-cleaning seats, which meant she didn't need to try to wipe her slime off.

She waved goodnight to one of the Earthlings who was also getting off at the same stop. The plump female waved at her, smiling. Then walked in the opposite direction to her home. Squip continued down the sidewalk, admiring the way falling raindrops glistened in the streetlights.

The sidewalks were empty tonight. Everyone was either home or still in transit.

Like many, Clarence worked mostly from home. He consulted with several different tech corps. Helping them make Earth more suitable for Setageans and other off-worlders.

Squip walked up to her two-story house. The bushes in front had been decorated with flashing colored lights. Christmas lights! The podlings had begun decorating. The lights lifted her spirits.

The front door flew open and Five and Six came outside.

"Can we put the Christmas tree up tonight? Can we? Can we?"

"I don't know. Let me eat dinner first," said Squip.

Five drooped slightly.

Eight, who stood in the doorway, said, "She didn't say, we couldn't."

He nudged Five and they bounced into the living room. Squip followed them inside. Six brought up the rear.

"Shut the door, please," said Two, who was sitting on the couch reading on her tablet.

Squip went back and closed the door. She walked into the kitchen.

Clarence was at the stove, making magic. The kitchen felt warm and smelled like tomatoes. He loved cooking and was always experimenting with Earthling food. She never knew what to expect. Which was a good thing in a mate.

"What are we having tonight?" she asked.

"A new dish. Lasagne. It was so much fun to make. You've got ten minutes before dinner."

He smiled at her and bounced over, wrapping her in his arms. She embraced him, their feelers entwining.

"Gross," said Ten, and got up from the kitchen table, leaving the room. "No don't go in there. They're hugging," he said, to one of the other podlings.

Squip laughed, but relaxed into the hug. It was good to be home. She loved her family.

Feelings of well-being and balance flowed through her. Making her feel stronger and more herself again. Sometimes going out into the world was difficult.

"Oh, I found something for you," said Clarence, he pulled out of the embrace and tapped on the wall screen.

"What?"

"I'll show you," He continued searching. "I was checking the local community center, looking for after-school classes for the podlings. I saw this and thought of you."

Squip looked at the screen. It was a class at the center. On Wednesday nights, which was the night between the two study group meetings. A dance class. It started tonight.

"But it starts tonight. In an hour and a half."

"They still have openings. You just need to show up. You can finish dinner by then and get to the class."

"But I need to spend some time with the podlings."

"They've all got homework to do. And if they finish early, we'll do some more decorating. They'll be fine. Go do this. It'll help with your presentation."

"You're sure? You're okay with putting them to bed."

"Yes. It'll help you meet more Earthlings."

"Okay, I'll do it."

Dinner was tasty, but rushed. She liked the stringy cheese. The podlings all behaved themselves. That didn't happen often.

She left the house half an hour before the class. Which was only around the corner. Squip bounced down the street, very excited about her first dance class.

The Echo Lake Community Center was busy. There were several different classrooms and a gym, where Earthlings played sports.

On the door was a notice about the Christmas tree lighting which would happen on Saturday. The family should come and watch.

Inside, Squip found the classroom with soft rhythmic music playing. There was only one Earthling inside so far. A female dressed in a turquoise outfit that seemed unusual for this time of year. It had no sleeves and was tight on her body and legs. This was covered by a transparent long skirt of the same color, but with silver glittery attachments. The female's feet were bare. She wore silver jingly jewelry on her wrists, ankles, ears and around her neck. Her long dark hair was loose and flowed everywhere.

"Good evening," said Squip. "Is this the dance class?"

The female looked like she couldn't think of an answer, but finally said, "Yes it is. Are you here to sign up?"

"I am. I don't know how to dance, not Earthling dances. I'd like to learn."

"Well then, welcome. I'm Yasmina. Have you ever seen Middle-Eastern dancing?"

"No."

"This is a class for beginners, so you're in the right place."

They held their wristbands close and the devices connected.

Squip's asked if it should pay the fee.

"Yes," she said.

"I've never taught an off-worlder before. I'll have to think about things differently. I'm used to working with human bodies," said Yasmina.

"We Setageans are very flexible. And we can jump higher than humans. There are some things we can't do that Earthlings can. I'll try my best to do what you teach. This is going to be such fun."

"Good. That's the most important thing, you know. If you're not having fun dancing, there's no point."

One by one, seven other Earthlings arrived to take the class. Each one stopped to pay for the class. Squip recognized the female who rode her bus.

"Oh hello," the female said. "You're taking the class too. I'm Kaya."

"I'm Squip, lovely to finally meet you."

"Well, I think it's time to begin. From now on, we'll start right on the hour, because we need to be out of here on time. I'm Yasmina. I've been dancing since I was a teenager and now, well, I'm quite a bit older."

The Earthlings laughed at the joke, which eluded Squip.

"We'll start every class with stretching out. Middle Eastern dancing used to be called belly dancing. But it's actually hip dancing. You'll need to be flexible in parts of your bodies that many of you have never used. For dancing, you'll want to be barefoot, so feel free to take any shoes off now."

The females who'd worn shoes took them off. Squip noted that many of them had their toenails painted in bright colors, just like Yasmina. She'd seen Earthlings with painted fingernails, but had never really seen any of their feet until now. They were curious beings, full of complexities.

Yasmina took them through a series of stretches. Squip could do a lot of them, but she had no hips, no waist and no upper torso. She had a roundish body, like all Setageans. So she did what was possible to follow along. It was easy to do wrist rotations, knees and legs. The same with arms, elbows and wrists. She had more flexibility there than many Earthlings. Her neck was so short as to be almost nonexistent, but it was flexible. And she had feelers to stretch too. A couple of the females had long hair they could whirl in the same way she could move her feelers.

After that, Yasmina turned up the music.

"I'm going to teach you some of the simple movements which you can use to build a dance routine. Eventually, you'll incorporate arm and head movements at the same time. This style of dance is all about isolating one part of the body from all the others."

Yasmina taught them one where they put a foot forward, then snapped the same hip forward above the foot. Squip had a tough time with that one. She finally found a way to thrust the center of her body forward over the top of her leg so that it looked almost the same. But Setagean bodies were wobbly. Where Yasmina's body snapped into place and stopped, Squip's kept jiggling.

Yasmina walked around the room and was helping everyone.

"I don't think I can do this one. I can't stop moving," Squip said.

"Not everyone can perfect every move. I've got one that you will excel at I think. Let me show you," said Yasmina.

She raised arms straight upwards and moved her hips in a

circle. During the circling, Yasmina bounced, just a little. Enough to make herself jiggle. Just like Squip.

"Oh, that's wonderful," said Squip.

She copied Yasmina, putting arms straight up and bouncing slightly to the beat of the drums.

Yasmina slowly brought her arms down, moving her hands in circles too. Squip did the same. The others in the class did the same. Two of the females were more cushioned than the others. They also excelled at this movement.

"This move is a really good way to shake out tension too. It's a nice one to do when you need to catch your breath," said Yasmina.

By the time the three-hour class ended, Squip had learned so many movements.

"Next week, we'll put them all together. In any order you want. So practice at home, every day. Stretch out first and then again at the end. Just like we did tonight," said Yasmina. "And next week, bring some scarves to tie around your waists. Or short skirts. Even a chain belt would work. Something festive. Also, bring a big scarf like this one. Something that's flexible and floats down nicely and I'll begin to teach you some veil work." Yasmina held up a transparent scarf that was as wide as her outstretched arms and went from her toes to her chin."

Squip was so excited. She'd had so much fun. In her short time on this planet, she hadn't spoken with many Earthlings. There seemed to be a barrier she couldn't cross.

But here, in the dance class, they all worked and laughed together. Earthlings treated her as a friend, not a stranger.

The next dance class was just as fun. Yasmina put on different music. Each one of them had to cross the floor, using at least three moves from the previous class.

Squip had found a jingly metal belt to wear around the middle of her body. And during her trip across the floor, she made that belt sing. At the end of her dance, everyone clapped for her, just as they had for the others.

She enjoyed seeing what each one of them did. The steps they chose to use and how well they did them. Completely unplanned. It gave her an idea.

Then Yasmina taught them how to use the veils. Squip had bought a large scarf made of thin transparent plasticloth, so she could wash her slime off it easily. She really enjoyed playing with the light green veil.

After they had finished stretching at the end of class, Squip stood up in front and said, "I have a question to ask all of you, if I could have a few minutes of your time."

"Go ahead," said Yasmina.

Squip explained about her study group and her presentation.

"When I came for this class, I was just trying to understand dancing. We don't dance much on Setagea, but maybe we should. It's wonderful. I had an idea. I'm wondering if all of you would come to my study group next week. It's very informal. We could do just what we did tonight and be nine ladies dancing. I could arrange for an Embassy van to pick us all up here. We could have so much fun."

"What night is it?" asked Kaya.

"Tuesday. Next Tuesday. We should leave here around five. Traffic's always terrible."

"Oh, a night out," said Yasmina.

"I can pick up any type of food we want and we could have a feast in the van," said Squip.

"What fun," said the redheaded shy female, whose name Squip had forgotten.

"Yes," said Jessa.

"I'm in," said Talia.

They were all enthusiastic about going. Yasmina suggested getting takeout from a Middle Eastern cafe she knew. She'd pick it up and Squip would pay her back.

Squip was so excited she could barely concentrate at work for the next several days. She practiced her dancing every night. In the middle of the living room, where the podlings had decorated every single possible space with Christmas lights.

Tuesday evening, she picked up the autovan from the Embassy parking lot and took it directly to the Community Center. Clarence and all eleven of the podlings were there to meet her. They embraced and Clarence gave her the jingly belt and the veil.

The others arrived and everyone met Clarence and the podlings. Who then went home to dinner and decorate some more.

Everyone climbed into the van and Yasmina passed around the various bamboo bags filled with food. Squip had never had Middle Eastern food and the flavors were spectacular. She needed to take Clarence and the podlings to that cafe to experience it.

Traffic was of course awful. They made it to the study group on time, although it took awhile to move all the chairs to one end. By the time, they finished doing that, the entire study group had arrived.

"Well, I see we have more guests tonight," said Lula. "Whenever you're ready Squip."

Squip went to the front of the room and stood. Her belt chimed whenever she moved. It was very pleasant.

The dancers stood together over to the left. Yasmina had

brought her music player. The dancers all had scarves or skirts or jewelry on and were ready to go. They'd stretched out while moving the chairs.

"I researched my verse: *On the ninth day of Christmas, my true love gave to me nine ladies dancing.* Some versions have the last four verses all mixed up. Others included lambs a-bleating, bulls a-roaring and bears a-beating. I didn't want to bring any bears or bulls. Far too dangerous for indoors. And lambs won't begin arriving until a few weeks from now. I chose ladies dancing. I know that some Earth cultures define ladies as a title of nobility. But nowhere could I find that Earthlings owned other nobles. So I chose to use the simple definition of female. I began to research dancing. The particular dance form I decided to present was not done in Europe at the time of the song. This is instead Middle Eastern dancing. It's so much fun. I've only been taking the class for two weeks now, as have the others, so keep that in mind. Yasmina, our teacher, has obviously been doing it for much, much longer. Together, we make nine ladies dancing. Yasmina, do you have anything to add?" asked Squip.

"Just that this is improvisational. You might see something like this at a family party or wedding dance. An actual performance would normally be highly choreographed and prepared for. This is spontaneous. Dancing should be fun and carefree. An expression of one's deepest self."

Yasmina started the music and the nine of them moved out into the center of the room, dancing around each other and sometimes coming close to colliding. Yasmina motioned them to follow her and they formed a circle. Each far enough apart to use their veils.

They copied Yasmina as best they could while moving in

a circle around the room. By the end of their dance, Squip wasn't the only one out of breath.

The study group clapped loudly.

"That was wonderful," said Lula.

Squip and Yasmina conferred.

Then Squip said, "We'd like all of you to join us out on the dance floor. Yasmina will put on some more music and we can all just jiggle and shake until we feel good."

Glitter was the first one out, but soon everyone had come out. Yasmina put on music and everyone moved around. The room was large enough they all had enough space. Even Niida and Martha. Squip noted they carefully kept to the outside edge and moved mostly their arms. Even Pyranz and Schooos joined in.

It was a glorious celebration. Squip's heart felt full. She could hardly wait to tell Clarence and the podlings about it. This was the way to get to know about Earthlings. And other beings too. Dance with them.

She would never have thought so before.

At the end of the song, everyone clapped.

The perfect ending.

And a new beginning. The trip home was just as fun as the one there. All of her dance class had fun at the study group. They thanked her profusely for inviting them. And Squip and her family got invited to three different Christmas parties.

She'd never been to a Christmas party. What fun this was turning out to be.

And all because of a silly song.

Her life was wonderful.

TEN LORDS A-LEAPING

It was a busy time at the Embassy, with many contracts being negotiated. A lot of Sartalans were emigrating to Earth, their sun was dying rapidly and life on the planet had become bleak.

Magwab was working too many shifts lately. Unlike most Embassy workers, security was ever-present. The security teams need to be staffed on nights, weekends and holidays, as well as during the normal workday.

Magwab sat in the food room and drank the last of his kilan, which was now cold. The strong sweet drink had needed more cream, but he'd only had a few minutes for his break.

He shoved down the feeling of sadness over missed companionship and friendship. He had his clan. Disconnected as they all were on Earth. There was no going back to Sartala and its death throes.

His clan should be enough. Except it wasn't. Earth had changed him.

Time to get back to work. He rubbed the fur around his

face and took the mug over to the counter, setting it into the cleaning alcove and closing it. The mug would wash itself and be put away he supposed.

Magwab adjusted the knife holster hanging on his hips. He flicked his long tail to release tension. He hadn't taken the long gun off when he sat down.

There had been an attempted break-in the previous night and everyone was on edge tonight. At least half of them hoping the intruder was stupid enough to return again tonight.

Magwab wasn't one of them. He was older, and perhaps wiser than those young cubs.

He stalked down the tunnel in complete silence. Two of the younger guards were talking. Gibbering on about some hot young thing.

Magwab snuck up behind them, taking the time to draw his knife. Then he grabbed the more aggressive one by the forehead, wrapping his tail around the cub's legs. Magwab held a knife at his throat. The cub kept struggling, pounding on Magwab's ribs, until Magwab drew blood. Magwab could smell the cub's fear, it was like the scent of rotten hania fruit.

The other one whirled and recognizing Magwab, stood up a little straighter. He flicked the rounded ears on top of his head forward in a gesture of respect.

The cub in his arms stopped struggling, slowly realizing he'd been caught by a superior.

"The two of you shut up and split up. Talk on your own hours," growled Magwab. "If I was the intruder, you could be dead now."

Magwab let go of the cub, who stumbled, trying to regain his balance. The cub's face was wrinkled with fury at being made to look stupid.

"Don't do stupid things," said Magwab. "Don't let living on Earth make you grow soft."

"There's no war here," said the cub, rubbing his bloody neck.

"There's always a war," said Magwab, repeating the Sartalan catchphrase.

"Not here on Earth."

"Humans are always at war. They just fight differently than us so you haven't seen it. What do you think last night was about? Look harder cub. And split up."

Magwab walked away from the two. Time to go downstairs to relieve Kantos, who was due for a break.

He ran down the exterior stairways. The cold wet air made him even more alert. He searched the exterior as he moved, but there was no one there, except Shirra, motionless and hiding in a dark alcove near the third floor doorway.

He flicked his ears at her in acknowledgement and she returned the gesture. Magwab ran down the last two flights and placed his thick clawed hand on the pad to open the lock on the first floor.

Inside was warmer. He shook the rain off his fur and crossed the floor to where Kantos stood behind a stone column.

"How has it been?" asked Magwab.

"All quiet."

"Good. Break time."

Kantos flicked an ear in acknowledgement and walked towards the outer stairway on the other end of the building. Magwab walked across the front entryway as if leaving to check the first floor. Instead he hid behind a stone outcropping.

The architect for this building had been Sartalan. She'd

created plenty of hiding places for security in the design. Clearly, she'd once been on security details and understood the importance of the Embassy.

It also left many places that needed to be checked for intruders on a regular basis, although all of the hiding places had cameras on them.

Magwab felt tempted to report the cubs now. There was a screen in the hiding spot. Perhaps he'd do it later. Best not to be distracted. There would be no successful break-ins on his watch.

He took a deep breath and settled in to observe. His hearing abilities increased, as did his sense of smell. His large eyes sharpened, easily able to see in the dim light. Nothing moved inside the walls.

Outside there was minimal traffic, either of cars or beings walking. His wristband read 3:27 a.m. Still too early for most embassy workers.

In another hour and a half the two head chefs would arrive and begin cooking for the day. Most of the work was done by machines invented by the Meazza and perfected by the Duveilians.

The night seemed to drag on. It was his last night of the week. The ambassador had returned from touring Earth two days ago and his large security detail was rested and ready to rejoin the Embassy security team. Magwab had four entire days off. Which hadn't happened for two months and a half.

He would need every minute of it to pull together his presentation which needed to happen on the fourth evening. He just hadn't had time while working so much and only having one day off in between each week. It had felt crucial to spend those precious days off with his clan.

After an hour and a half where nothing stirred, Magwab

left the hiding spot and walked the first floor. Checking all the rooms and hiding places.

He stopped at a screen and checked the surveillance system. Nothing caught on camera except the guards. Everyone had reported in, on time even, and they found nothing out of the ordinary.

At 6:50 a.m. the next shift of guards arrived and checked in. By 7:03, Magwab had surrendered all his weapons, made his report, picked up some containers of freshly cooked food for breakfast and was out the door, picking up an Embassy autocar from the parking lot. The other guards had stayed to eat at the Embassy.

The trip back to the Caves, as they were affectionately called, took an hour. He ate the dipploa meat spiced with the flavors of Sartala. Sina, a hot seed, burned on his tongue and the back of his throat. It was complemented by mooslir's complex sweet-woody flavor.

Rain darkened the gray sky, another late fall day here on this part of Earth. Which didn't bother him at all.

He'd been surprised to find the darkness had an effect of some humans. They were born on this planet and a fairly adaptable species.

After eating, Magwab began using the screen in the auto-car. After looking for a few minutes, he decided to avoid the entire nobility topic. There had been no nobility in this part of Earth. He'd never be able to bring one to the group. They were extinct.

Great Britain had held onto the titles the longest, but when the Earth began to fall apart and most of their land had been flooded, they had completely abandoned their former government, along with nobility. Most of whom were wealthy and had fled to higher ground in other countries.

Then he found one little piece about an old vid, *Lord of the Rings*. That looked promising. It had been made into a series of holos he vaguely remembered watching back on Sartala. Just before coming here. Before that, a series of movies. Long before that, a series of books.

By the time the autocar pulled up at the Caves, Magwab had a plan. He reserved a car to pick him up at noon. Four hours of sleep would be enough.

Magwab entered the large stone building—this one carved out of the side of a hill. There were only two ways in or out. The front, plus an underground tunnel that came out the other side of the hill, known only by Sartalans. Both entrances were heavily guarded. Sartala commanded all the land surrounding and on top of the hill. It was heavily planted with trees and bushes, although there were trails if one knew where to look.

Inside, Magwab moved through the cool dark tunnels. One chamber had a fire going. Several Sartalans of his clan sat around a fire, drinking kilan. Magwab didn't stop.

Another room had cook fires going and some Sartalans sitting around eating. Magwab could smell the roasting meat and the rich tangy tingami paste it was being basted with. He kept moving, grateful for having already eaten.

He found a cavern, artificially created and reinforced, that had space. It was generally used only by those on night shift. The beds were lined with cave moss imported from Sartala, as well as fern fronds collected on the hillsides above.

Magwab fluffed up the bedding and curled up in one of the alcoves, the earthy scent make him feel comfortable. He fell asleep immediately.

Four hours later, he woke.

Magwab walked through the bathing room, rubbing soap

into his fur, rinsing it beneath the weeping ceiling. Then he dried himself near a fire, rubbing oil on the soles of his feet and the palms of his hands. He brushed the fur on his body, arms, legs, face and tail.

He ate a quick meal of chicken, mixed with a few vegetables and a broth. It wasn't as spicy as he liked it, but the food filled his empty belly. He drank a mug of hot kilan in one gulp.

The embassy autocar pinged his wristband that it was out in the parking lot. Kilan went outside and climbed into the small car. He set the destination for a hotel near the old airport.

The airport was now a museum, replaced by many smaller regional airports. With new tech arriving from all over the multiverse, long distance travel had changed. Airplanes had been replaced by flyers which were much smaller, faster and more efficient.

On the two hour drive Magwab watched holos for his research. By the time he arrived at the hotel, it was 2 p.m. Not as early as he would have liked, although festivities were scheduled round the clock.

A big sign out front read: *Welcome Lord of the Rings Conference*. Three humans walking through the parking lot wore costumes from the holos. Magwab recognized Tom Bombadil, Arwen and an orc. An unlikely combination.

He got out of the car and told it to park. Then walked into the hotel. There were tables staffed with more people in costume in front of a large sign that read *Lord of the Rings Con Registration*.

Magwab headed to the tables.

"Great costume man," said the human, who began to register him for the conference.

"Thank you," said Magwab, not wanting to insult the human.

Magwab paid with his wristband. Then held it up to sync so that the schedule and locations could be downloaded.

"You're good to go," said the human. "Have fun."

"Thank you, I will."

As Magwab walked away, one of the other humans said, "Dan, I don't think that was a costume. I think that's an off-worlder."

Magwab grinned. He walked through the crowd of mostly humans. Nearly all of them were in costume. Some from the *Lord of the Rings* holos. Others from holos he recognized, but couldn't name.

His first stop was the dealer's room. It was filled with people selling all sorts of things. Fake weapons and a few real knives and swords which were highly ornamented. His fingers lingered over one of the swords. Fine work indeed. There were booths with costumes of all sorts. Other booths sold jewelry, candles and holos. A couple even sold paper books, some old, some new ones made from bamboo paper.

Magwab bought a handmade black leather bag ornamented with an intricate design. It was meant to be worn across one's body and had a strap that was just long enough for him.

Then he went back to the book stand and bought a new edition of *Lord of the Rings*. He'd found reading human books was quite entertaining.

Magwab stood along one wall watching the parade of beings pass. Some had clearly used enhancements others not. He'd never seen such a wide range in the shapes and sizes of humans. And most of them were dressed in costumes. Some of which Magwab recognized, many he didn't.

A short round human dressed as a hobbit kept passing by and looking up at him. On the third time past, the male came over and stopped in front of him.

"Who are you?"

"I'm Magwab."

"I don't know that character."

"I'm not a character. I'm an off-worlder. From Sartala."

"Oh, I'm sorry. I didn't recognize you. I've never seen a Sartalan before."

"Not a problem. We're new here on Earth."

"So, what brings you to the con?"

"I wanted to see cosplay. It's a long story."

"I've got time," said the male. "I'm Jason."

The male held out his hand uncertainly. Magwab shook it and Jason grinned at him. Magwab told Jason his problem.

"Hey man, I got 'cha covered. First, we gather the tribe."

Jason spoke into his wristband.

"Okay, they'll meet us at Devi's booth. We gotta get you a costume."

Magwab followed Jason through the crowd, which had only gotten thicker with bodies. Then he lost sight of him.

Magwab felt uneasy being jammed in so tight with others. He couldn't protect himself. A knife could come from anywhere. Then he saw Jason waving to him from a booth over on the side.

Magwab wove left through the crowd. Finally, he was clear and inside the large booth. Which was also full of humans, but not like the aisle.

"Is it always this crowded?" asked Magwab.

"Nah, a panel probably just got out. It'll thin out. It's close to dinnertime. The crowd will dwindle."

Magwab looked around. The large booth, three booths

actually, was stuffed with clothing. Not like he saw humans who came to the Embassy wearing. These looked like a mixture of historical clothes he'd seen in photos or old vids, and holo costumes.

When he turned back to Jason, Magwab saw six other males. Then seven. Then finally, an eighth one squeezed out from the crowd. Every single one of them in costume.

"Good, we're all here," said Jason, surrounded by the eight males. "This is my friend Magwab, Magwab this is Jon, Caleb, Esa, Sinemet, Max, Ian, Frank and Liam."

"Cool costume," said Max.

"It's not a costume doofus," said Jason. "He's from Sartala, an off-worlder. Who needs our help."

"What can we do for you, dude?" asked Jon.

Jason explained the situation.

"We can help with that," said Esa.

"I thought so," said Jason. "We've got nine members of the Fellowship here. Let's add a tenth. What shall we make him?"

Fellowship sounded familiar to him. Then Magwab realized they were all dressed as characters from the Lord of the Rings holos. And they were costumed perfectly. Looking almost exactly like the characters.

"I don't really fit in," said Magwab. "No one in the holo has striped fur."

The nine males looked at each other and said in unison, "Sauron."

"It's perfect," said Jason. "Completely covered with armor, no one will see your stripes, just the height. Are you okay with being the baddie?"

"Can you find armor to fit me?" asked Magwab.

"Devi," said Jon, touching the sleeve of a female with

long dark hair and a brightly colored dress. "Can you fix our friend up with a killer Sauron costume?"

Devi walked in a circle around Magwab, obviously assessing him. She held up her wristband and he knew it measured his size.

"Yes. Are you willing to tuck that tail inside the pants?" she asked.

"I can do that. My tail's flexible. Although I'll be slightly off balance."

"No doubt the armor will throw you off balance even more," said Devi. "We can also give you a long cloak to cover the tail. I'm warning you, under all those layers you'll be hot, especially with fur. Okay, I'll gather some things up and you can try them on. I don't have pants as long as your legs. We'll need to cover them with tall boots, provided I have boots that fit you. Your feet are small for your height, I just might. Give me a few minutes and I'll get things printed up. You all can help him find some black pants and a shirt for a base. Then go check the boots. And I'll need a deposit."

Magwab held up his wristband and she took the payment. Then she motioned to two other people in the booth. Probably asking them to cover for her. She disappeared behind a curtain.

Jason took the largest pair of black pants off a rack. Jon did the same with a black shirt. They led Magwab to a curtained alcove and he went inside with the clothes. Jason pulled the curtain in front of it.

Magwab heard Jon say to the others, "This is gonna be fun. We've never had a Sauron before. He'll need a sword. Liam, go over to Nasir's booth and see if there's something there."

Magwab has only worn clothes twice before. On Sartala,

as he trained to be an embassy worker, they'd tried on clothes from a couple of the worlds which required clothing for everyone.

Here on Earth, clothing use was determined by the part of the world one was in, but off-worlders were exempt from clothing requirements.

The pants were made of a stretchy fabric and fit, although he had to roll the waistband down below his tail, if the tail was out. He coiled his tail up flat and tucked it inside the pants. Then pulled the shirt over his head. It was a tight squeeze. Sartalan heads were wider than human ones.

He looked in the mirror. If his lower legs and feet, hands, neck and head were covered, no one would know he was a Sartalan. Except for the height.

"How does it look?" asked Jason.

Magwab pulled the curtain open.

"Dude, you're going to look spectacular," said Ian.

Jason nodded and grinned.

"Okay, let's try on boots," said Jon.

Magwab followed them to the far corner of the booth. A salesperson wearing an elf costume glanced at Magwab's feet.

"What type of costume are you making," the male asked.

"Sauron," said Jon. "Devi's printing the armor now."

"So plain black boots?" asked the male. "I'll ask her."

He went behind the curtain.

Magwab noticed the aisles had cleared somewhat. People had gone to dinner.

Jon said, "Devi makes the best armor of anyone here. She prints up leather armor. Real leather, not that plastic crap that degrades so fast. You just have to keep it fairly dry. She did Frank's armor too, although he doesn't have as much as you will."

Magwab nodded.

He looked at his companions. Jon was costumed as Gandalf, although he'd taken off the pointy hat and his beard was short. The beard looked real, although dyed gray. Jason was Frodo. Caleb was Sam. Esa had curly hair and a baby face like Pippin. Max, a little taller was Merry. Sinemet must be Legolas, his ears were pointed. Frank wore a highly ornamented costume so was probably Boromir. Ian was shorter than Jason and had pointed ears and a beard, that made him the dwarf Gimli. Liam was the only one missing. He also had a beard and was dressed plainly. That would make him Aragorn.

The salesperson returned with a large bag and a pair of socks. Magwab remembered humans wore them beneath shoes. He slipped the black socks over his feet. They felt strange, but warm.

The male had pulled two boots out of the bag. They were tall, almost knee high. He unzipped them and handed one to Magwab. Then pointed to a chair.

Magwab sat and began to put it on.

"Other foot," said the male.

Magwab switched feet. The boot felt tight and cramped at first, but his feet adjusted. He could wear them for a few hours. He zipped it up and put on the other boot. Then stood.

"How do they feel? Your feet are fairly wide. I got the widest ones we have."

"I think they're good," said Magwab, moving around slightly and balancing on one foot, then the other.

The clerk was waving his wristband over the boots. He nodded.

"What else do you need?"

"A large long black cloak," said Jon.

The male led them to a section of cloaks. Jon began looking through the rack.

Devi came out from the back, with an armload of stiff black objects.

"Oh, that looks great," she said, to Magwab. "Let's do the lower legs and thighs first," she said, wrapping bands of black leather around them and snapping them closed. The leather had been polished with a silvery substance making it look metallic.

After that Devi showed him how to put on the lower torso armor. It wrapped around his waist and hung to mid-thigh. Then the lower arm and upper arm guards. Finally, she wrapped a shell-like object around his ribs and over the shoulders. She showed him where it fastened on the side and just below the shoulders in front.

Devi stood back and looked.

"Dude, that is so awesome," said Jason.

"Gives me shivers," said Jon.

"Gloves and helmet," said Devi. "Are you going to be using a weapon?"

"Magwab, do you have enough credits for a sword?" asked Jason.

"Yes."

He didn't have to ask how much the sword was. His credits had been stacking up for years. He never spent them. One of the good things about being an embassy employee. Every need was taken care of.

"Okay," said Devi. Digging through a container full of gloves. "These might do. See if they fit. They have a good grip.

Magwab pulled them on. They were also silvery-black

and looked like chain mail, but they were fabric. The gloves were thin and flexible, almost like skin.

"Okay, let's try the helmet on. I put in lots of vents, but it'll still get hot inside," said Devi.

She handed him the helmet. It was light, despite the tall rigid spikes on top. Magwab pulled it over his head. Somehow, she'd managed to make it perfectly balanced. It didn't feel top heavy.

He could see out the eyeholes and breathe out the mouth and nose.

"Wow," said Devi. "That's spectacular, if I do say so myself."

"You've outdone yourself, Devi," said Jon.

"How does it feel?" she asked.

"I don't have any problems," said Magwab.

He squatted down. It was cumbersome, but possible. He wouldn't have wanted to work in it. The hearing wasn't perfect, but it would do nicely.

"Look in the mirror," said Devi.

Magwab walked over to the mirror. It wasn't him, it was Sauron from the holo.

Devi slipped a black and silver metallic cloak over his shoulders and tied in it front.

Liam had returned and said, "I found the perfect sword. Holy crap, that's amazing!"

"Ring! He needs a gold ring!" said Jon.

Devi found the perfect ring, even in the right size.

Devi took photos of all of them. Magwab paid the balance. He stuffed the boot bag into the black leather bag he'd bought earlier and snapped the strap on, over the armor and beneath the cloak. It blended in perfectly.

They went off to buy a sword. Humans in the aisle parted

where he walked. Some just felt the menace of his costume. Others looked and pointed.

At Nasir's booth, there were ten swords. All of them were blunted and not for fighting with.

"I don't sell sharp swords at cons," he said. "These are ornamental."

Two were the same size, large for humans. One of them looked perfect with the costume. Everyone pointed to that one. A scabbard and belt were found and the transaction finished.

"Okay," said Jason. "Let's go have some fun."

"Dinner," said Caleb. "I gotta keep up my Hobbitness."

"Pizza, our room," said Esa.

"Right," said Max.

"Magwab, do Sartalans eat pizza?"

"I've never had it. We eat anything if it has enough meat."

Esa walked off by himself and began speaking into his wristband. When he'd finished, Esa joined them.

"I ordered six large pizzas. They'll be here in ten minutes. That's forty credits each."

Everyone touched their wristbands to his. Magwab had to pull his glove back to find the wristband.

"Let's go walk through the lobby," said Jason. "Have some fun for five minutes, then head up to the rooms."

They left the dealer's room and Magwab followed them out into a wide spacious area. One entire wall of windows looked out over the parking lot. He could see it had grown completely dark outside.

Jason said to him, "You've seen the holos, right?"

Magwab nodded.

"So all you need to do is to look menacing. If we pretend

to attack you, draw your sword and play at attacking us. Remember that we're humans and you're really big and strong, so don't really attack us, or even touch us with the sword. Just pretend, shake it and look menacing. Like the actors on the holos. Got it?"

"Got it," said Magwab.

They came to a section of the lobby that wasn't as crowded. Off to one side of the space, the others separated from him and facing him, pulled their weapons.

He roared and pulled his sword.

The noise drew the attention of passers-by. They stopped and a crowd began to form.

"Though shall not pass," said Jon.

The others began mock threatening him.

Magwab grinned beneath his helmet.

He laughed out loud and said in a voice eerily like the holo actor who'd played Sauron, "None of you can stop me, try as you will."

The crowd had grown quite large. Many of them held their wrists up to shoot vids. The tribe formed a line, bowed, and motioned for Magwab to join them as they posed. He sheathed the sword and stood behind them.

After the photo opportunity, people came up to talk to them and compliment them on their costumes. Then they walked farther through the lobby and repeated the scene.

Devi had been right. The helmet was hot. Beneath his fur, Magwab sweated.

"Okay, that's enough," said Jason. "Let's go back to the room for dinner. I'm starving."

"I swear, you eat twice as much when you're Frodo," said Jon.

"I know. If I did him all the time, I'd weigh 300 pounds."

They all crammed into an elevator. Magwab had to bend over, as he did for human doorways and some buildings. He couldn't possibly fall over in here, they were jammed in so tight. The rooms were on the twenty-third floor.

It was a relief when the door opened to their floor and the others began to stream out. He followed them down the hall and into a room. As soon as they were inside, the others began removing cloaks and weapons.

Magwab took his helmet off and felt cool air flow past. It was such a relief. He took off his cloak, sword, ring and gloves, putting them in a pile in the corner. Then removed the leather bag, adding it to the pile.

There was a knock on the door.

"Pizza," said Esa, walking to the door.

"I'll get the sodas from the fridge," said Liam. He went through an open doorway into another room.

"Do you want to take off more of your armor?" asked Jason.

"I think I'm fine," said Magwab. "We're going back out again, right?"

"Heck yeah," said Jon. "The night is young."

"There's a costume contest tonight. And a dance. Although I don't think you can dance in that helmet. Better to take the costume off altogether for that," said Jason.

The scent of spiced meat filled the room. Esa brought in flat boxes and set them on the small table and another piece of furniture. He opened the boxes and handed out thin round pieces of stiff bamboo paper. Liam brought in ten plasticans and set them near one of the boxes.

Magwab did what the others were doing. Put triangles of the flat bread on the paper and grab a plastican and sit down. He watched the others eat and copied them.

He could taste the meat, but the overwhelming flavor was rich and fatty. Jason told him it was cheese. Made from cow's milk. Magwab decided it was just as satisfying as meat.

He didn't like the soda. It was fizzy and tasted strange.

After eating, they began to dress again.

"Okay, we've got to check in for the contest. Then we'll hang out and wait for our turn to go on. I think we're somewhere in the second half of the contest. So an hour or more. There's a new emcee. We don't know how fast or slow they'll be. Magwab, you might want to leave the helmet off until just before we go on," said Jon.

He nodded, relieved.

"Clean up before we go, okay?" asked Esa. "We have to sleep here tonight and I don't want to smell pizza all night long."

The others began bending the boxes and taking them out to the hallway to put into the compost receptacle. Liam gathered the plasticans to dispose of in there as well.

Magwab picked up his belongings. He put the leather bag on and tucked the cloak inside it. Then strapped the sword around his waist.

"Magwab, do you have a place to crash tonight?" asked Jason.

"I was planning on going home."

"You live close by?"

"No. Two hours."

"That's a lot of travel time, dude. You won't have time to sleep. You can stay here if you want. We can get another rollaway bed. We're all sharing two rooms. The more of us there are, the more money we save."

Magwab hadn't even considered staying at the hotel. It would be the smart thing to do.

"That would be good," he said.

"Jon, order another bed," said Jason. "The tribe that plays together, stays together."

Magwab felt a sense of warmth. Clan. He hadn't had two clans since leaving Sartala and he so missed all of them, dispersed so rapidly throughout the multiverse.

The wait for their turn in the contest was long. They sat in a large windowless room with all the other contestants. Magwab only recognized a few costumes from holos.

Liam told him that many of the costumes were from books, some from manga, others from ancient vids. Magwab was stunned at the work which had gone into many of the more extravagant costumes. They were more elaborate than the ones he'd seen walking around the con. Looking at them was like a feast.

The intervening time was spent talking. Jon told him about other local cons the tribe was going to. Magwab put the schedule in his wristband. He'd need to see if it was possible to arrange the time off. He had a lot of vacation time coming, having never taken one.

"If you're coming to more cons, we can even choreograph a few fights. That would be fun," said Jon.

Their time was coming up. The tribe put on their remaining costume pieces.

Jon pulled him aside as they waited backstage and whispered last-minute instructions. Magwab nodded and then they were on.

The others went on first. The area backstage was dimly lit, but Magwab could easily see. The stage was bright. He gave his eyes a second to adjust to the brilliance. The others were pretending to wander as if searching for a path.

Magwab stalked onstage and roared at them. The others turned and gathered into a clump, protecting Jason.

A female in a bright blue gown stood on the edge of the stage. She spoke, announcing them.

"And now we have the Fellowship of the Ring and Sauron."

Magwab stalked around the group, sword drawn and looking for an opening. Jon moved outward, sword in one hand and staff in the other.

Magwab slowly struck at him with his sword. Jon countered it and they held that pose for ten seconds so people could take photos.

Then Jason nodded and they all formed in a group to pose. Magwab could see into the audience now. It was darkened. There were hundreds of beings. Mostly human, although many were in costumes, so they might not have been.

Jon was grinning, obviously pleased. Magwab hadn't had this much fun since he'd come to Earth.

They returned to the waiting room, although everyone kept their costumes on. Magwab only removed his helmet.

Most of the contestants had been on now and the results had been announced. Many of those who hadn't placed had been let go.

Those who had were waiting for the end and the judging results to be announced. Magwab didn't quite understand how these things worked, but he felt content to wait. There was nowhere he'd rather be.

Then Jon said, "We're on. We'll just go up and take a bow."

Magwab put his helmet on and followed the others to the backstage area. All the other contestants were called first.

"Lastly, here are our Grand Prize Winners: The Fellowship of the Ring and Sauron," said the female in blue.

Magwab followed the tribe onto the stage, where they went to stand in the center. The audience was standing and clapping. There were whistles and other vocalizations, which Magwab decided were compliments.

The tribe joined hands and bowed as one. After a few minutes the stage lights dimmed and everyone left the stage.

Jon had been given a gold and silver oblong statue and an envelope. They went to the elevators and joined the masses of crowds waiting for the elevators. It seemed to take forever.

Finally, they jammed into an elevator and returned to their room. Then they took off their costumes. The humans changed into different clothes. Magwab simply shook his fur dry. All of his costume, except the helmet, fit into the leather bag and the boot bag. He piled them neatly in the corner.

They went downstairs to dance the night away. Magwab had never been to a dance with humans. It felt wonderful to move and stretch and be himself, as they were being themselves.

He remembered Squip's presentation and the dancing. This felt similar. Just jiggling to the music, she'd called it.

The next day they wandered the halls in costume again, performing scenes for people. Having their costumes admired and doing the same for others in costumes.

Many had noticed Magwab at the dance the previous night.

"You should come up with a cosplay where you can just be yourself. That fur is spectacular," said one male.

Magwab nodded, grinning and unsure how to reply.

The entire weekend had been such a revelation. Including

the discovery that many humans snored in their sleep. Sartalans never did.

They parted with a promise to meet at 5 p.m. on Tuesday at a cafe. Magwab had reserved an autovan that would take them to the study group.

Magwab slept late into the day on Monday and again fitfully on Tuesday morning and afternoon. Trying to recover from the con and get his schedule back on track. On Wednesday, he would be back on the nightshift again for the week.

The autovan took him to the Hobbiton Downs cafe. It was a small brick building jammed in between two other older stone buildings. Structures from before the big quake devastated the region.

Magwab left his costume in the autovan and went inside the cafe. Most everyone was already there. Only Jon was missing.

"Magwab!" said Jason.

"Good evening," said Magwab, sitting in a small wooden chair. They were all small to him.

"How are you today?"

"Tired. I didn't sleep well trying to get back onto a night schedule. And I was too excited about tonight."

"Well, five of us are still tired from the con. We all worked Monday and Tuesday. The other four of us have con crud," said Liam.

"Con crud?"

"It's like a cold or flu that gets passed around at cons. People gather and someone's always sick. That gets spread around and if you've spent the con overdoing things—partying, staying up late, not getting enough sleep—you get sick. Con crud," said Esa.

Magwab's stomach rumbled loudly.

"Well, nothing wrong with your appetite," said Jason. "Let's order. We can order for Jon and if he doesn't get here in time to eat, we'll pack it up for him to eat on the way."

Magwab decided on one of the specials, roast pork with cherries and bourbon sauce. He drank water and listened to the others talk, amazed at how close he felt to these special humans.

The meal went quickly. He worried about Jon. They needed to leave at 6 p.m. to get to the study group at 7. They were relatively close, but traffic was awful tonight. As usual.

They packaged up Jon's meal, a burger Jason called it. Magwab paid for their meals to thank them for coming to his study group. They were nearly out the door when Jon rushed in.

"Bus broke down," he said.

His face was red, breathing ragged from running.

"Just in time," said Jason. He held up a bag and said, "We got your dinner, you can eat on the way. Catch your breath."

Jon nodded and followed them out into the rain.

The autovan pulled up and they piled in with all their gear, finding seats.

The drive to the study group seemed fast, mostly because Magwab spent the entire time putting on his costume. During that time, Jon managed to eat his dinner, change into his costume and organize the presentation.

"Okay, we're ten lords a-leaping. So we'll need to leap. I did some quick research today while I took a shift at the front desk, at the library. It was a slow day. One of the things cited was Morris Men. I'm not sure about that, couldn't find out if there were Morris Men or their equivalent in France. It's not clear where the song came from anyway. Too many changes in the lyrics. But it gave me an idea. Morris Men do steps and hops or leaps, and smack sticks together. I think we should do the same with our swords. I came up with a simple routine we can do. It's very repetitive, so we can pull it together in five minutes if we try. Is there a place we can practice before your group Magwab?"

"The building has a hallway where we can practice out of sight of the group arriving."

"Good. We'll do that then," said Jon.

"This is gonna be such fun," said Liam.

"I am so grateful to have met all of you," said Magwab. "And for your help with this."

"Thanks for being our Sauron," said Jon. "How's it looking for the next con?"

"I've got all of them scheduled as vacation. My supervisor was stunned. I've never taken vacation before," said Magwab, laughing.

"Never? You must love your job. What do you do?" asked Jon.

"I'm a security head for the Sartalan Embassy."

"Wow. What does that mean exactly?" asked Jason.

"On the shift I'm scheduled for, I'm responsible for making sure all the others are where they need to be and doing their job. Basically, endless rounds of walking the entire building."

"Does anyone every try to break in? I wouldn't. You Sartalans look way too fierce, even without the Sauron costume," said Jason.

"Yes they do try. There are many more deadly off-worlders in the multiverse than us. And none of us are immune to death."

The autovan pulled up at the destination. They left their belongings in the van and went inside. Magwab grinned. He loved the way they all looked when they were in costume. He'd left his helmet off for now.

He pointed towards the hallway and the others went around the corner. Magwab popped his head into the room. Niida and Martha were already there.

"If you would be so kind as to move all the chairs to the edges of the room, I would be grateful," said Magwab.

"Oh, you have a costume on," said Martha. "I can't wait to see what you have planned."

"It's going to be fun," said Magwab. "I'll be back when it's time to begin."

Then he went down the hallway. Once he found the others, Magwab set his helmet on the floor.

Jon had them line up into two rows and then showed them the steps and the sword moves. Magwab was paired with Jason.

"Careful with that big sword of yours," said Jason.

The human was only half-joking, Magwab could tell.

"I'm always careful of weapons," he said. "I know humans are very fragile."

They walked through the steps and swordplay at a slow pace. Then speeded it up to real time.

"It's three minutes to seven," said Jon. "We should stop and rest. So we're fresh for your group. Sinemet and Frank, you two need to coordinate your swords better. Caleb don't worry as much about the steps as getting the sword movements right. I think we're as good as we can be for now."

Magwab nodded and said, "I'm going to go to the group and do the first part of my presentation. Then we can dance. Why don't all of you follow me in? Get a sense of the space."

"Sounds good," said Jon.

Magwab picked up his helmet and led the way into the

room. Everyone else was already there. Even Lula. Most of them were sitting in the chairs around the edge of the room. Niida and Martha sat on the floor, as was their custom.

"Perfect timing," Lula said. "And I see you've brought guests. Do you need anything from us or are you ready to go."

"I'm ready," said Magwab.

He walked to the front of the room.

"My verse was *On the tenth day of Christmas my true love gave to me, ten lords a-leaping*. I began to research and decided not to use the meaning of the word lord, which describes noble males. I knew I could never find nobles in this area. They never existed in this part of Earth. And even in other areas, nobles and royalty have mostly become extinct. Like Squip, I found no references about nobility owning other nobles outright. I chose to portray the meaning of human male. Then I found the holos for *Lord of the Rings*, which I'd watched months ago. And a reference to a *Lord of the Rings* Conference. So I set off to explore that. Which is where I met my friends here. They helped me find a costume. So together we are Lords of the Rings. And we will be leaping for you."

Magwab nodded to Jon, who walked out into the center of the room, followed by the others. They lined up in the same positions as out in the hall. Magwab put his helmet on and all of them drew their swords.

Jon said to the Lords, "We'll do our routine twice. On three. One, two and three."

They began. It went well the first time. On the second time around, Frank and Sinemet got their swords tangled and fell off tempo. Caleb tripped over his own feet, did a tumble and was back up again with a speed and grace Magwab hadn't known the human possessed.

They somehow got back on track and ended well.

The audience clapped and clapped.

"Oh, that was wonderful," said Glitter.

"I adore all of your costumes," said Asoona.

"You look like you walked straight out of the holos," said Daisy.

"Wonderful," said Lula. "Simply wonderful. I'm so impressed with how creative each of your presentations have been. I hope you're all learning a lot."

Magwab beamed and removed his helmet to cool off.

"This was really fun to do. Thank you, all of you," he said, to everyone in the room.

"Can you teach us the dance?" asked Lula. "But maybe without the swords."

Magwab looked at Jon.

"We'd be delighted," said Jon.

The study group came out to the center of the room and soon they were all dancing and stumbling about. Magwab left his helmet off, it was just too warm in the room.

After the group ended, Magwab and his friends piled back onto the autovan and headed back. Magwab insisted on dropping each of them off at their homes or their vehicles.

Finally, only Jason and Jon were left. They lived in the same apartment building.

"You're coming to the next con, right?" asked Jason.

Jon seemed to be eagerly waiting to hear his answer as well.

Magwab decided the humans were feeling uneasy about his commitment to their tribe.

"I wouldn't miss it for anything in the multiverse."

All of them grinned.

"Good. We'll be in touch about transportation. None of

us has a big enough car to hold everyone and all our stuff. So we usually take several cars," said Jason.

"Why don't we all rent an autovan? I'd bring this one, but Embassy vans aren't able to leave the city, except for diplomatic events. But we could rent one."

"None of us have enough credits to reserve one," said Jon. "We've tried pooling out money, but the deposit rate is phenomenal."

"Let me try," said Magwab.

"You're on," said Jon. "That would be great. We could make up some songs as we ride."

Humans were full of surprises. Magwab was going to enjoy being part of their tribe. It gave him a sense of relief to have two tribes again.

He felt warm and at peace with himself as he waved good night to his new friends and the autovan turned towards home.

They would all meet again soon.

ELEVEN PIPERS PIPING

Glitter stood in front of the screen at the multilevel front desk in the lobby. It allowed Meazza to speak with other beings and be at face level with them. He stood on the highest section.

Far too many beings equated size with superiority. They were fools. The Meazza were small, but more intelligent than many, who were much larger. Known for their inventiveness, Meazza had become a hub of new tech.

New tech had been used in this lobby to impress other beings. The entire building was responsive to its inhabitants.

The temperature in each room automatically adjusted to the needs of the majority in the space. A room filled only with Sartalans would cool itself to their optimal temperature. One containing Tolpians would warm to a balmy condition. The Meazza preferred it even warmer and drier. For a room containing beings from multiple planets, the room could be divided into differing temperature zones.

Light was adjusted as well. Even though the ceiling was transparent plastiglass, a Meazza invention, New Seattle often didn't have enough sunlight for many. The lighting made up for that on the dark days of rain. Again, light was adjusted to the majority of those within the room.

Meazza was a wealthy planet. Everyone who could, worked and shared with those who couldn't. Together they were Nest. The wealth dripped from this building.

Not wealth in human terms. There were no gold jewels here.

Wealth for the Meazza meant that no one wanted for anything. If one Meazza didn't have food, the Nest was all the poorer for it.

Meazza desired comfort to do their work. They loved work. Unlike most humans, Meazza chose their work. It wasn't dictated by economics. If they decided their work no longer suited them, they moved to a different profession.

Caring and teaching nestlings was the highest calling of all. Nestlings were the future. They would create new inventions, keeping the Meazza alive and wealthy.

Glitter rustled his hot pink wings, stretching them out. Enough. He knew enough about pipers and what eleven pipers piping might mean.

Their presentation was on Thursday. Three days away. And still, they hadn't been able to agree on a plan.

Mush flew in, back from her break. She landed on the short end of the platform.

The front door swooshed open and a cloud of Meazza flew in on their way to their posts. Four others walked in, arguing about the need for a greater connection with the Duveilian Embassy. They were followed by a Catalpan on her way to translate the signing of a contract.

Tinkerbell and Shoe hovered outside the doors. Politely

waiting until everyone else had passed through. Then they flew in and landed on the platform

"We need to make a decision," said Glitter. "Where's Blueberry?"

"She's trying to find a new name," said Shoe. He didn't meet any of Glitter's three eyes.

"We agreed to not change our names until the study group had ended," said Glitter.

"She can't help it, she's restless," said Tinkerbell.

"We all are," said Glitter. "But we agreed."

"We gave our word, I know," said Tinkerbell. "But, she's going through some changes. Be patient with her."

"What changes?" asked Shoe.

"I'll leave it up to her to tell you," said Tinkerbell.

Glitter felt annoyed. As leader of their cloud, he should have been informed first. But Tinkerbell and Blueberry had been nestlings from the beginning. Their relationship went back farther in time.

Blueberry had been gone a lot lately. Did that have something to do with it?

"What if we can't decide?" asked Mush.

"Then one of you gets to stand up in front of the study group on Thursday and tell them we have no presentation. And make all Meazza look inept," said Glitter.

"It's not that dire," said Tinkerbell.

"It is. We need to decide on a presentation while we still have time to prepare," said Glitter.

"He's right, this time," said Mush.

Shoe fluttered his wings in agreement. Tinkerbell flicked a front leg in annoyance. Which meant she still disagreed, but would participate.

Blueberry finally arrived.

"Sorry I'm late," she said, out of breath. "I was helping set up a contract negotiation."

"That's not your area," said Glitter.

"The Meazza, whose area it is, was out sick today. They needed help. I was there, so I helped."

Glitter let it go. Blueberry looked out of sorts. He couldn't pinpoint what was different, but she wasn't her usual buoyant self.

"We're going to make a decision on our presentation. Now. We have to present three days from now," said Glitter.

"Okay," said Blueberry. "What are we choosing to do?"

Glitter continued, "Well, there's Tinkerbell's idea, which is wonderful. Learning to play the pipes would be fun, but we only have three days. I don't think it's enough time. There's Mush's idea, which is great, but not very practical. And Shoe's idea which only made sense to him and no one else."

Shoe fluttered his wings as if to say it didn't matter.

"I think we should do a variation on Tinkerbell's idea. Not learn how, but hire them."

Tinkerbell's eyes brightened to a spring green.

"I like that," said Shoe. "But what do we do during the presentation?"

"Dance," said Tinkerbell. "I've seen humans do it. We can learn that in three days. And our movements will be different because we have six legs, not two."

"Okay, let's vote," said Glitter. "Everyone who's willing to do Tinkerbell's idea, flutter your wings."

Everyone fluttered.

"Okay, Tinkerbell go find someone to hire. Shoe find out about dancing. Mush and Blueberry you're in charge of any costumes we'll wear. Coordinate with Tinkerbell on that."

"What are you going to do?" asked Tinkerbell.

"Worry. And coordinate everything, including travel and credits."

The others flew off to begin working. Glitter took a deep breath and began his own work. He reserved a large Embassy autovan. And added up all their credits, hoping they had enough.

The man in the song must have been very rich to give all those gifts to his intended. Especially if, as someone had suggested, that each day built on the previous ones and included all the previous gifts as well as the new ones.

Glitter spent the rest of the afternoon worrying, while doing front desk work. Signing in and directing strangers to their destination. Greeting tour groups, many of whom were human conservation groups interested in how human buildings could be designed better. They'd come to see the Meazza Embassy for inspiration and were led around by an engineer and an architect.

Just before work ended, Tinkerbell returned.

"I found a group. They're happy to come, for pay. But they want to make sure that they're who we want. There's a rehearsal tonight. I told them we would all go listen."

"What time?"

"4 p.m."

"That's two hours. We'll need an autocar."

Glitter tapped on the screen, reserving one.

"I hope we can get there in time."

"I told them we might be late, depending on traffic."

"Okay, spread the word to the others and tell them to wear some woolies. We meet here the minute work ends. You and someone else can get some food from the dining room for us."

Meazza needed to eat many small meals. Their metabolism was fast, especially under warm conditions.

Glitter finished his closing work, including a report of the day, which would be accentuated by security vids of the lobby. One never knew when such things might be needed.

Then, after the front doors had been locked and the lighting dimmed to reflect the building's closure, Glitter flew to his cubby and pulled out some woolies.

The Embassy provided them for all Meazza during the cool fall, spring and winter months, calling them woolies after some quaint human phrase. They were soft clothing that could be worn over a Meazza torso, legs and head, but which left wings exposed. They were light enough to fly in and not too cumbersome to wear for hours on end. They did indeed feel cozy.

Soon, all five of them were in the back seat of the autocar, sharing a meal of steamed Calan snails.

"Delicious," said Mush, closing her eyes in bliss.

The autocar was driving across town, taking side streets. The rehearsal space was nearby, but even on side streets, traffic was moving at a crawl. The freeway would be worse.

Finally, the vehicle's navigation program switched it to streets with only one lane, in an attempt to avoid the jam ups. By the time the autocar pulled up to the rehearsal, they were only five minutes late.

"Whew," that was close," said Shoe, flying out the now-open passenger door, into the rain.

"Park," said Glitter, to the vehicle. "Be back at 5 p.m."

The autovan closed the open door, locked all the doors and drove off to search for a parking space.

The brick building looked old. The five of them hovered beneath a fabric canopy, trying to open the heavy door. They fluttered their wings, trying to dry them off. In the end, it took all five of them to pull the door open. They flew in quickly.

A loud wailing sound came up the stairwell from the basement. They flew down to make sure no one was dying.

The only door in the basement was closed, but lighter in weight and easier to open.

A brightly lit room was small and filled with humans. One of them was blowing into a musical instrument creating the wailing sound. Several others joined in. They seemed to be adjusting their instruments.

So those were bagpipes. They sounded awful. Perhaps the noise would improve. Glitter didn't think it would possibly resemble anything he considered music. Did humans have inadequate hearing, too?

A human with silver chin hair saw them when the door opened. He walked over to them as they hovered near the door. Were they in the right place?

"Good evening," said the human. "Who's Tinkerbell?"

"I am," she said, moving forward. "And this is Glitter, and Mush and Blueberry and Shoe."

"I'm Ian. I'm sort of in charge here. We're just getting ready to play, all this rain means we need to retune. If you'd like to take a seat somewhere, maybe over there. We'll be ready to play in a few minutes."

"Thank you," said Tinkerbell.

Glitter flew in the direction the male pointed. The others followed. They sat on a long empty table and watched the musicians intently.

Glitter noted that there were twelve humans in the room. The wrong number. Perhaps they could ask one of them not to play. The humans were trying not to stare at them. Glitter had grown used to being stared at by humans. Off-worlders were still relatively new here.

"How are the two of you doing with costumes?" he asked Mush and Blueberry.

"If we're dancing, we need something light," said Blueberry. "We want to be able to move and fly."

"I think the best we can do is wrap something light and colorful around out legs. Or perhaps our torsos. We're still working on it," said Mush.

"Shoe, what have you found about dancing?"

"I found several old vids and some new holos. I don't know if we can learn it in two days. But we can try. We'll need to watch them and practice."

"Tonight then. When we get back to the nest."

One by one, the musicians stood up and went to the other side of the room. All except one of the females. She remained seated, manipulating her lower legs and feet in a strange manner.

Then the leader, Ian, said, "And a-one, two and three."

They began to play music. If that's what it was called. Each one blew into a tube that led to a bag beneath their arms. It had three other tubes sticking out the top and one at the bottom. The bottom one had holes in it. The humans' fingers moved back and forth over the holes and their mouths blew into one of the top tubes.

The sound was deafening. Glitter had seen several of the musicians putting little colored plastic things in their ears.

Tinkerbell was fluttering her wings in excitement. When the musicians paused after the song, she spoke.

"Ours will be the loudest presentation."

Glitter flicked a front leg in agreement.

The musicians began another song. This one was even louder, if possible, and more rousing.

The last female got up and stood in front of them. She began to bounce up and down, moving only her legs. Every now and then, she would raise her arms straight up and continue moving back and forth across the floor in the same up and down manner.

It took Glitter a while to understand she was dancing. This was completely unlike the dancing that Squip had done. Was this the way humans danced to bagpipes? It looked very complex.

This song was shorter than the first one. As the musicians tended to their instruments, making adjustments and the dancer bent over in a strange manner, Ian walked to the back of the room.

"Well, what did 'ya think? Is this what your were looking for?"

Tinkerbell looked at Glitter. He cocked his head in a yes. So did all the others.

"Yes," said Tinkerbell. "That was perfect. Can all of you come on Thursday? We can reserve an Embassy van to pick you up."

"We're in. Half the payment in advance," said Ian. "All of us have bills to pay, instruments that need repairing."

Tinkerbell spoke into her wristband and held it up to Ian's.

"Perfect. I'll make sure everyone has the details. What time do you need us?"

"We'll pick you up at 5 p.m.," said Tinkerbell. "It'll probably take two hours to get there. The study group is about an hour, perhaps longer, that's up to you. The drive back will be shorter. If you want to order food to eat in the van on the way over, it would be our pleasure to pay."

"You sure about that? Pipers have large appetites," said Ian.

"We would be honored to feed you," said Tinkerbell.

"Okay. I'm sure it will be much appreciated."

"I have a question," said Shoe. "Can we speak to your dancer?"

"Certainly. Fiona," said Ian, waving to her.

She walked over to them, moving in a manner that was unlike most humans. She seemed powerful and strong, completely present in her body.

"What can I do for you?" she asked.

"Could you teach us some of the basics of the style of dancing you were doing?"

"I could try," she said. "It's obviously going to be more complicated for you, with six legs."

"We'd love to learn what we could," said Shoe. "We'll pay you extra for teaching us, just an introduction tonight. We need to leave in forty-five minutes to get to our study group. And then we'll practice on our own tomorrow. Then Thursday, we'll show our study group what we've learned."

"Okay, let's go out in the hallway and I'll teach you what I can in forty-five minutes."

They flew behind her out into the large hallway which seemed to comprise most of the basement. She had them line up and showed them some steps.

Glitter copied her, doing the same things with his three left feet as she did with her one. The same on the right side. The others appeared to be following along similarly. Except Blueberry, who'd always been uncoordinated.

"Now, add a little bounce with each of those steps," said Fiona, demonstrating.

Glitter couldn't seem to make the bouncing part happen.

"How about using your wings?" said Fiona.

He tried it again, and with his wings was able to bounce.

"Oh, this is fun," said Tinkerbell.

Then the pipers began playing again, the sound somewhat diminished through the closed door.

"Okay, now let's try to follow the rhythm of the music," said Fiona.

Glitter began dancing. Following the same pattern, using the same steps with the same sequence and bouncing.

"Good, you're all doing really well," said Fiona.

They kept repeating the dance steps, over and over again, until the song ended.

"I think I have it," said Blueberry.

"Good. Do you want to try another step?" asked Fiona.

"Yes," said Shoe.

She taught them another sequence and then the pipers began another song.

Glitter tried hard to match the rhythm of the music. It took awhile, but he was finally able to do it.

This song was faster, as was the step. By the end of it, he was out of breath and exhausted.

His wristband pinged that the autocar was waiting.

"Time to go," he said.

Shoe said, "Just let me pay Fiona. Thank you so much. We'll all practice hard tomorrow and be ready on Thursday night."

"I can't wait to see you all dance again," Fiona said, holding her wristband to Shoe's. "The most important thing is to have fun."

"That was exhausting," said Blueberry, once they were in the autocar. "I sure hope tonight's presentation is rousing. Otherwise, I might fall asleep."

All the next day, Glitter spent his time at the front desk dancing. His legs ached from the strange movements. Every time he saw one of the others, they were doing the same thing.

By the end of the day, he'd decided that those who had early presentations had gotten off lightly. With each presentation, the bar had been moved higher, as humans would say.

The five of them practiced the steps back at the nest, in their own section. There was no music, of course, but they could imagine.

Finally, Blueberry said, "I'm done. I'm too tired and can barely move."

"You're always tired these days," said Shoe.

"What if I am?" she snapped.

"Stop," said Glitter. "Both of you. Go get some rest everyone. Tomorrow's our big day."

As they went to lie in the soft bedding and sleep, Glitter noticed how much his legs ached. All that dancing.

He woke the next morning, with his legs unrested. He'd dreamt all night of dancing. His limbs probably twitched all night long.

Today was the day. He roused the others. Blueberry was already up and eating in the common hall. Glitter sat beside her and they shared a long strip of simbonna fruit.

"What's going on with you these days?" he asked.

"Do you really want to know?" she asked.

"I wouldn't have asked if I didn't."

"I'm full of eggs."

"Aren't you too young for that?" asked Glitter.

"Apparently not," said Blueberry, her head cocked to indicate he'd asked a foolish question.

"You're right. Well, that changes things. Will you stay in the pit with them?"

Some adults always stayed at the pit, separating eggs from the grubs and ensuring both were kept safe. Meazza metamorphosed before they reached their adult form.

"I don't know."

"Well, let us take care of you. Don't push yourself too hard. I wish you'd let us know earlier."

"I don't want any special treatment," said Blueberry.

"You're body is going through special changes. You need to be treated differently right now. I can't even imagine the extra burden on your system. Does the other Meazza know?"

Blueberry indicated not.

"You should tell him."

"I can't. I found out after he returned to Meazza."

"Well, he can't be involved in the grubs' lives then. Was it Darren, Obsidian, Apple?"

Blueberry sighed and flicked her front leg in acknowledgement.

"It will be instructive to the others to have someone in our hatch full of eggs. I can't speak for the others, but if you should decide to stay in the pits with the eggs, I will join you. You shouldn't be left alone to do all that work. Turning the eggs. Keeping all the grubs away from the sleeping eggs. It's important work."

Blueberry paused from eating and stared at him, her wings fluttering slightly.

"Thank you. That would be comforting to have my hatch-mates there."

They finished eating and gathered the others, who were

eating a piece of calina meat. All of them caught the first auto shuttle to the Embassy.

Glitter couldn't practice dancing while greeting beings at the front desk. His legs ached too much and he could barely put any weight on them.

He hovered above the platform. Then found his legs doing the dancing steps anyway. Mush joined him and began doing the same thing. They were perfectly synchronized. Then Shoe flew in and danced with them.

An hour later, Tinkerbell returned from an errand and saw them.

"Oh, that is spectacular. Let's all do that tonight. My legs ache from overuse."

"This will make the dance ours," said Mush. "Humans can't do this."

Tinkerbell joined them and later, Blueberry. They added in wing gestures and a perfectly matched flip at the very end.

A crowd had formed in the lobby of the building. Mostly Meazza, but some of the other off-worlders. A few humans were there too.

After the last flip, when Glitter stopped to rest, so did the others. The crowd applauded. And they hadn't even heard the pipe music that ran through Glitter's mind.

Glitter looked at the others and beamed. They bowed, in human fashion, to the crowd. And flicked their front legs in gratitude.

They left the Embassy early in an auto van and drove directly to the pipers' rehearsal space. They arrived with fifteen minutes to spare.

Ian was already there. He began loading up some cases.

"I've got three sets of pipes here. Some of the band didn't

want to haul them to and from their work. We'll need to pick up the food. I knew I couldn't carry all of it," said Ian.

It seemed to take forever until all the humans showed up. Only one of the pipers was really late, by five minutes.

"Roads blocked by an animal rights demonstration. Downtown buses couldn't get through," said the red-faced male. He was panting, breathing hard. "Had to run for it."

The van drove to the restaurant and Ian and Fiona went in to pick up the food. Tinkerbell went with them to pay for it.

They were on the road again by 5:20 p.m. Just over an hour and a half. Glitter hoped for no accidents on the freeway. It wasn't raining at least, even if it was dark. Humans didn't see well in the dark.

The humans ate tacos, burritos and quesadillas. They'd ordered extra and shared them with the Meazza. Glitter ate a few bites, but didn't feel very hungry. He handed the extras to Blueberry, who ate the rest of the taco eagerly. Soon she'd double in size and be unable to fly.

But there was an accident. It plugged the traffic flow up for a good half hour and then they were past it. Glitter's stomach felt tied in knots.

The Meazza busied themselves with twining the blue and green ribbons around their legs, as costumes.

They arrived at the meeting place at two minutes after seven. Glitter rapidly flew out of the van and pressed the button to open the wide door.

Once inside, he flew into the room where the group met.

"I would like to give our apologies for lateness. We had to work around the humans' schedules and then there was an accident on the freeway. Please give us a few more minutes to set up and we'll be ready to give our presentation. Thank you," he said, to the study group.

"Is there anything we can do to help?" asked Lula.

"Perhaps you would be so kind as to move the chairs to those three edges of the room and sit at the far end," said Tinkerbell, who'd flown in, followed by Mush.

The study group began rearranging chairs as all the pipers and Fiona came in. Shoe came walking in with Blueberry. Not flying.

"Is everything all right?" asked Glitter.

"Maybe too many tacos," said Blueberry.

"She couldn't fly out there in the wind," said Shoe.

"Can you fly in here?" asked Glitter.

"Give me a minute," said Blueberry.

"If not, you can dance on the ground. We could join you."

Blueberry waved a leg at them, in annoyance.

He went to check on the pipers. They'd taken off their heavy coats and gloves. Their instruments had been removed from cases.

Glitter noticed they all had uniforms on. Black shirts and blue, green and black fabric wrapped around their waists and over their shoulders forming a cape. Black socks and shoes. Their knees were bare. In this cold weather. They all wore a similar small cap of black. So small it couldn't possibly keep anything warm.

Fiona wore a black shirt and a similar piece of fabric around her waist. With black socks up to her bare knees. And flat black shoes, but no cap.

Ian said, "We're almost ready, just need to take a couple of minutes to tune up."

"Okay, I'll begin our talk," said Glitter.

To the other Meazza, Glitter said, "We'll go through the routine once on the ground, then those who can, will fly. Blueberry, why don't you stand in the middle. That way if you can't fly, there will be balance."

Blueberry flicked a leg indicating acknowledgement.

The Meazza lined up in front of the pipers, who were at the far end of the room. Glitter stood facing the study group.

"Good evening, and thank you for your patience. Our verse is: *On the eleventh day of Christmas my true love gave to me, eleven pipers piping.* When preparing for our presentation, we chose the oldest meaning of the word. Bagpipe pipers. We found this wonderful pipe band, here," said Glitter. "The New Seattle Pipe Band."

At that moment several of the pipes let out loud discordant noises as they began to tune up. The sound echoed off the bare walls and windows of the room. He also heard an extremely loud Meazza belch. Probably Blueberry. She'd feel better now.

Glitter said, loudly, "Bagpipes are quite loud, so even in the large hall of an estate house, they would have been overwhelming. You'll get a small taste of their music after they finish tuning up. Fiona will dance for all of us. And we Meazza will endeavor to join her in our own way. She's had years of experience, we've only had a couple of days, but it is so much fun. Whenever you're ready Ian."

Glitter waited. After a few more loud noises. There was a short silence and then the band began to play.

Glitter recognized the song from their rehearsal, the slower song. He and the others began to dance. Out of the corner of his eyes, he could see the others moving along with him and behind him, Fiona traveling back and forth across the floor between them and the pipers.

They did once through the routine on the floor. Then all of them, Blueberry included, took to the air. Performing their routine twice over, until the song ended.

Then they landed. The study group applauded and the band and Fiona bowed. Glitter and the others bent their front legs and dipped.

Then the band began their faster song. Glitter and the others worked hard to keep up. They did the entire song in the air, it was easier that way.

When the song ended, Glitter was out of breath. He could tell Blueberry was done.

The study group clapped again and Glitter turned to the band and standing on his back legs, rubbing his front ones together, creating a squeaking noise that indicated thanks. The other Meazza did the same.

"That was wonderful," said Lula. "I've never heard bagpipes. They're quite loud."

"They were once used in battle," said Ian. "To rouse the warriors to fight."

"And to frighten the enemy," said Fiona.

"Well, that was quite something," said Lula.

"And you are quick studies," said Fiona, to the Meazza. "I just taught you those steps two days ago. I love how you translated them to flying. It was wondrous to watch."

"A job well done," said Fiona.

Some of the other members of the study group had moved forward and were talking to the pipers, wanting to understand how the pipes worked. There were several demonstrations going on at once.

Glitter beamed. Their presentation had been a success.

Blueberry came and stood by him.

"Feeling better?" he asked.

"Yes. I should have told all of you when I first found out. I was too shocked to think clearly."

"Well, it has turned out wonderfully, don't you think? Hatches stay together and take care of each other," he said.

"Thank you," she said. "I was worried that none of you would understand."

All of them were there now, standing close and relaxed. Calm, now that their challenge had been met. The evening had been perfect.

Glitter was reminded of the most important thing, together they were strong. Truly, they were Nest.

TWELVE DRUMMERS DRUMMING

Vert tapped his green fronds on the table, only half listening to the Ambassador ramble on about her current plans. She often had these long meetings which took everyone's time and accomplished little other than a feeling of bonding for those forced to sit through them.

The large room was brightly lit and warm, like all of the Camassan Embassy. Camassans could eat food, but gained most of their nutrients through photosynthesis. He'd once heard a human rudely call him a walking plant, which Vert supposed from their point of view, he probably was.

Two of the people at the table had their heads down as if looking at their screens. He knew they were dozing. Jella was busy planning her joining celebration with Mallen. Two others were drawing pictures on their screens while pretending to take notes.

His fronds felt dehydrated. His rhizome tense and anxious.

He really needed to be working on his presentation for the study group. He'd been researching and planning it since the very first week of class. But then as each of the others had presented theirs, Vert had felt the pressure to make his better and more elaborate. Time had not been his ally in this endeavor.

His very-complicated presentation was due tomorrow night and everything was going wrong. He needed to get out of this meeting and speak to everyone involved, making sure that each piece was still on track.

The longer the meeting went on, the more scarlet his pinna turned. Each leaflet more stressed than the minute before. Finally, three hours later, they were released.

Vert fled to an empty workspace and closed the door, locking it for good measure and drawing the shades on the plastiglass walls and door. He left the shades on the wall facing the outside of the building open to let in light.

He contacted as many humans as possible by text. It was faster. Three didn't communicate that way, so he opened up a holo line for the first human and waited to see if they responded.

"Hello," said Jack.

"Jack, good afternoon. This is Vert. I just wanted to make sure we were still on schedule for my presentation tomorrow night."

"We're good to go, as long as that van arrives to pick me up."

"I'll double check and make sure it will pick you up at 4 p.m. I'll see you at 6:30 tomorrow then. And thank you," said Vert.

"Pleasure doing business with you," said Jack.

The line closed.

Vert took several minutes to check his van reservations. Three vans had 4 p.m. pick-ups. Five vans were scheduled 5 p.m. pick-ups. Three vans for 6 p.m. pick-ups. And one human was providing their own transportation. Everything was going well there.

He put several fronds over his face. This was going to cost him so many credits before it had all finished. He might have to take out a loan. But the glory of Camassa was on the line.

Vert opened up another line.

"What d'ya want?" asked the bearded disheveled male.

"I just wanted to make sure we are still on schedule for tomorrow night."

"Oh yeah, right. We'll be there. The van picks us up at 5, right?"

"No. 4 p.m. Traffic is always terrible at rush hour. The van will be there at 4 p.m."

"Okay. We'll be ready." The line closed.

Vert sighed. It would be a miracle if everything went right.

He turned the mister on for a few seconds and refreshed himself.

Then he returned to the desk and opened another line.

"Yeah," said the deep voice.

"Hello, this is Vert. I just wanted to confirm that you're still coming tomorrow night."

There was silence.

"For the presentation. This is Millie, right?"

"Oh wow. I'd forgotten all about that. I tripped and fell. Broke my arm two days and the pain meds are something else. Mostly for my back, hurt that too. But I'll see if I can get a friend to help me haul stuff."

"The van is scheduled to pick you up at 5 p.m.," said Vert.

"It can haul a trailer, right? For my critter?"

"Yes, I've confirmed that," said Vert, but I'll double-check.

He made a note on the screen.

"I'll call if my friend can't help. I sure could use the credits though. Won't be able to work for a while."

"Let me know as soon as you can," said Vert, but the line was already closed.

Should he make other arrangements? No, that human had been the only one he'd found.

The sun went behind clouds and the room darkened. He wasn't sure if it would be possible to make it through the winter here on Earth. At least not this far north. This was his first winter on Earth. And New Seattle was dark.

Even during daylight hours, so much of the time the sky was completely clouded over and the light was the same as just before dusk. He'd been careful to increase certain nutrients and decrease others. As well as spending more time under artificial light, but that didn't seem to help.

He wanted to curl up and just go completely dormant. Some Camassans did that. And some never came out of it.

To do so would be to let the study group down. They'd all been so kind to him. Even the ones who ate plants.

Vert upped the carbon dioxide levels in the room and breathed deeply. He'd get through this.

His wristband vibrated. Four texts had replies. That left five unanswered. He'd wait a little longer. Humans were slow to respond at times. Such busy lives.

Another vibration. A text from Siffha.

Come see me in my office. Now.

That couldn't be good.

He went anyway.

Vert stood outside her closed office door. What could he

possibly have done wrong now? All his tasks were on schedule.

He touched the door and it slid open.

"Good afternoon, Vert. Have a seat."

"Thank you."

"So, you haven't been here very long. How are things going?"

"Good. All of my projects are on track and I've been making a list of new ideas."

"Fine. How's your personal life?"

"Good."

"I notice that your credits have taken a real hit in the last month or so. There's hardly anything in your account. That doesn't sound *good*."

"Oh. It's for a study group I joined. I've been paying for, um, parts of a presentation that I'm doing tomorrow night."

"That's one expensive presentation."

"Yes, it is. But I'm the only Camassan in the group and I wanted the other beings to have a good impression of us."

"So, you feel you're representing Camassa in this group?" asked Siffha.

"Yes. There are eleven other beings, twelve if you count the instructor. We're all from different planets. It's a very diverse group."

"Interesting. What sort of a presentation is it?"

"Well, it's a human study group. The instructor decided we should understand human holidays. Christmas is coming up and she chose a song, *The Twelve Days of Christmas*. Each of us has been assigned to present a verse. The other presentations have been spectacular. Mine is the final one."

"So, you're determined to outdo all the others."

Vert looked down. Was that so wrong?

"Yes."

"Well, more power to you," said Siffha. "Are you filming it? Where's the presentation at?"

"I hadn't planned on filming it. I think I'll be too busy organizing everything. It's at the Firs at Douglas Creek. Where I live. In our little community center."

"Oh, I know that place. I had a friend who lived there. What time?"

"7 p.m."

"I think I'll pop in. I'd like to see what you've got planned."

"Wonderful," said Vert, brightening to pretend it was.

Even though it wasn't. It was awful.

He didn't need more pressure.

"Great. I'll see you at seven tomorrow," said Siffha.

Dismissed, Vert went to a workstation with a screen and pretended to work on his projects, while waiting for texts to come in.

By the time the workday ended. Three more texts had come in. Things were on track. Things that had gone badly wrong over the weekend had reversed themselves.

That left two outstanding texts.

Before he left the Embassy, Vert slipped into shoes and wrapped up in a plasticoat, for warmth, and caught a shuttle home.

Squip texted him. *Can hardly wait till tomorrow to see what you come up with.*

She was kind. He knew she was trying to send encouragement. She'd already finished her presentation and it had been brilliant. Vert worried the entire two hour trip home.

The Firs at Douglas Creek was a development with indi-vidual homes set in a woodland. The landscape was maintained by employees and used only native plants, to encourage wildlife. The residents weren't allowed to plant anything or tend to the grounds. They could walk the forest paths, but were instructed to leave any wildlife alone. Pets of any type were not allowed. Violations of the rules could get one evicted. Most of the residents were human, although a few off-worlders lived there.

Vert had wanted to live among humans. He'd decided it would help him understand them better, which would enhance his work at the Embassy.

He got off the shuttle and walked the darkened sidewalks. They were dimly lit by streetlights festooned with flashing colored lights. Someone had put the colored lights up today. He had no idea why, but they looked cheerful in the darkness.

Sprinkles of rain dripped down. If it had been warmer, it might have been soothing. Tonight called for a long hot bath. If his condo was closer, he would have used the hot tub at the recreation center. But it was at the far end of the complex and in this weather, he'd cool off too much walking back home.

He put a frond on the DNA pad at his condo and the front door slid open. Inside, he pressed a button and it closed behind him, locking.

His house felt warm. The heat had been turned on automatically when it sensed his impending arrival. The humidity was perfect. Vert hung the plasticoat on a hook to dry.

He went to the main room, kicked off his shoes and sunk his feet into the nutrient bath. Vert's feeding tubes descended from his legs and opened. Sucking the nutrients into his body.

Basking in the heat, warmth and artificial light, Vert recovered somewhat from his harrowing day. Wishing, once again, that he'd stayed on Camassa.

The beautiful breathtaking light. The always-warm temperatures and perfect humidity. The peace and solitude. Serenity was an everyday occurrence there.

Why had he thought it would be exciting to make his mark on the multiverse? Why had he longed for adventure?

He stepped out of the nutrient bath and set it to refresh. Then checked his texts again. One more had come in. They were on track. Only one human hadn't replied. And then there was the one who'd fallen. So two potential problems.

He should search for substitutes. Tonight. Just in case.

Vert went to his screen and began going through his notes. So far, he'd found no one else who could supply what the non-responding human could.

But the song lyrics had variations. He searched again. There. He could switch things out if necessary. Use the variation.

His phone rang, startling him. No one ever called.

"Hello."

"Vert? Millie."

"Good evening Millie."

"My friend can come help me out. I'll be there tomorrow night. The van comes at what? Five you said?"

"Four. The van will pick you up at four. And it has the type of trailer hitch you specified."

"Okay. We'll be ready."

"Thank you so much," said Vert.

He sighed with relief. Then called the human who hadn't answered the text. There was no answer. He left a message, asking for a confirmation that the human was coming tomorrow night.

Then he spent the next hour on the phone trying to arrange a backup. He finally found someone who could come at the last minute and who would wait until 3 p.m. tomorrow for confirmation they'd be needed.

Vert transferred a deposit to their account, shivering at the hit his credits were taking. He scheduled another autovan pickup and made a note to cancel if it proved necessary.

He refused to think about Siffha coming to the presentation. He spent every week at the Embassy trying to impress her. Why did she have to haunt him during his time off?

He spent the rest of the evening practicing his talk and going over his notes. Making sure every last detail was covered.

It was past midnight before he finally decided to rest. Vert walked over to the nutrient bath and stepped in. Having completely forgotten to take a hot bath like he'd planned. The nutrient bath was the best he could do.

He stood in it and told the room to darken. And slept fitfully all night long. Siffha's laughter in his dreams was the worst of it.

Vert woke as the room brightened. He didn't feel rested. He stepped out of the nutrient bath and into a warm shower. At least he was hydrated.

He checked his messages. The human still hadn't responded. Vert called to leave another message, but got one in return.

"This number is out of service."

Now what did that mean? He definitely couldn't count on that human. He felt relieved there was a back up plan. He needed to remember to cancel the autovan for them.

Then Vert put on the plasticoat and shoes and walked to the shuttle stop.

It was another rainy gray morning, but not cold like last week had been. The humans who lived in the complex were mostly silent, as usual. Only two of the females were talking.

"Two more weeks. At least I've got my shopping done. Well, the presents. I'm still wrapping them. But there's all the grocery shopping, cooking and baking and decorating left to finish," said the tall one.

"I know. Every year I say we should do less. And every year it gets blown out of proportion again. My entire family's coming. And a few friends. I realized last night that I'll need to make six pies," said the plump one.

"Same here, except it's my partner's family. Twenty-seven people will be crammed into my house for the day. It's gonna be one huge turkey."

The shuttle arrived and everyone got on board.

Did they all celebrate Christmas? And feast together?

Camassans tended to be more solitary. Only coming together to share work. They left their families early in life.

What would it be like to have family or even other Camassans crammed into a house his size. Twenty-seven of them. He shivered. It would be horrible.

The next day at work rushed past as he focused on his project. It was a plan about putting together a team of off-worlders from different embassies to go out and visit human schools.

The human never returned his call or answered, despite Vert calling every hour. At 3 p.m. he called the backup human and told her the van would be there in an hour.

"I'll be ready," she said.

"I can't tell you how much I appreciate this. Thank you so much."

"You're welcome. Credits on my account will be quite sufficient."

Everything was on track again. He canceled the spare autovan, saving a few credits.

Then stood in a nutrient bath in the main room for fifteen minutes. Then at 4 p.m., he wrapped up in the plasticoat, put on shoes and left work.

The autocar waited for him outside and he went straight to the Firs. He wanted to be the first one to arrive.

The sun was setting behind the dark clouds. It hadn't even bothered to come out today.

There was clearly an accident on the freeway already, somewhere up ahead. Vert wished he had enough seniority for a flying car. But he didn't.

The commute took a full two hours. He spent the entire time checking for messages and going over his notes. By the time the autocar dropped him at the community center, it was 6 p.m.

A beaten and abused older vehicle was parked outside the entrance. A burly bearded male was hauling a large metal cage out of the back end, letting it slide to the ground. Much squawking and hissing ensued. He shut the vehicle and walked to the entrance, pulling the cage.

The cage had wheels and rolled along behind him. Pale shapes milled around inside, jostling each other.

Vert came up behind the male, who stood at the door, probably trying to figure out how to open it.

"Oh hey there, little fella. I didn't see ya there. I don't understand all this new tech."

Vert pressed the button and the door slid open.

"Well, look at that," said the male.

Vert followed him and his birds inside, not sure exactly which ones they were.

Vert hung his plasticoat up on a hook in the hallway and slipped off the shoes.

"Hope I'm in the right place," said the male. "Didn't know how traffic was gonna be, so I left real early."

"I'm Vert. Yes, you are. I think you're the first to arrive. I'll have everyone set up in the hallway down there. Around the corner and out of sight. Then when it's their turn, come into that room," he said, pointing. "I want to surprise the study group."

The man raised his eyebrows and said, "This is gonna be fun. I like surprises."

Then he hauled the cage down the corridor and around the corner. Vert hoped everyone else would arrive early too.

He showed the male where to wait. Then went to the classroom and turned the lights on. Vert began dragging chairs to the edges of three sides of the room. It was hard work. He left two large open spaces for Niida and Martha, who always sat on the floor.

He'd just finished when someone entered the hallway outside.

"Hi," asked a breathless male voice. He was carrying a heavy square box. "Am I in the right place for the study group?"

"Yes, you are. Let me direct you to the hallway around the corner. That's where I want everyone to wait. I'm Vert."

"Hey Vert, I'm Burt. We rhyme."

Vert laughed, trying to approximate a human laugh. It came out like a strangled gargle instead.

Vert walked down the hallway and Burt followed along, breathing heavily.

"Now what have you brought?" asked Vert.

"Swans. Bloody swans. Well, not bloody. You know what I mean."

"All right. If you'll just put them down here." He pointed to a spot in the hallway next to the cage of other birds. "I'll have you come into our classroom, one by one."

Soon, others arrived and Vert placed them into a line, checking his wristband to make sure everyone was in the right order. His mind reeled with details and worry.

He took a break and went to the classroom. Niida, Martha and Asoona had arrived.

"Good evening," he said. "I'm here. Just preparing my presentation."

"Good," said Martha. "Are the chairs where you want them?"

"Yes, I already arranged them."

"You're organized," said Niida. "The parking lot is filled with autovans from the Camassan Embassy. How many guests are in your presentation?"

"A lot," said Vert. "It sure doesn't feel like I'm organized, it feels like complete chaos."

Just then a screech came from outside the door.

"I'd better get back."

He ran down the hallway to find that Burt had uncovered his box. The dancers had arrived and one had stuck a finger in the cage, trying to pet a swan.

The female was waving her hand around wildly.

"Here, let me see it," said Burt, finally grasping her arm. "It's just a little blood. Not a terrible wound. More bruised than anything."

"I've got some disinfectant," said one of the other dancers, rummaging around in her bag.

The dancer pulled her hand away from Burt, glaring at him and the swans.

"You're the dancers. I'm Vert. If you'll come over here, this is where you'll be in the order of presentation."

The dancers stopped stretching and picked up their belongings and followed him.

"This is nuts," said one of them, in a high-pitched voice. "What kind of presentation is this again?"

"*The 12 Days of Christmas* song," said Vert.

"And what are you dressed up as?" she asked.

"I'm not dressed up. I'm from Camassa. I'm an off-worlder."

"Oh. It's still nuts," she said.

Vert went to assist more newcomers.

He glanced at his wristband. Three minutes to seven. Only one group missing. That was Millie. He hoped she was coming. He pinged the autovan and it replied, "We are in heavy traffic."

They were still seven minutes away.

Vert went to the head of the first group in line.

"Oliver, isn't it?"

"Yes, you've got a good memory."

"My head's spinning with names. In a few minutes, I need to go in and begin to give my presentation. There's still another group on their way. The autovan says they're about seven minutes away. When Millie gets here, could you direct her for me? She needs to stand between the swans and the dancers. In that open space."

"Got it. Millie between the dancers and the swans."

"Thank you. I'll be out once I've done my introduction. Then it'll be your time to come in."

"Vert, this is gonna be fun. If you're not having fun, you're not living. Keep that in mind."

"Thank you. I will. Although, I think it'll be more fun when it's over."

Oliver laughed.

Vert went inside the classroom. Everyone was there, except Lula. Siffha waved a frond at him. She was talking to Magwab. Vert returned the wave.

Just then Lula burst through the door, her face red from running. She lugged a large heavy bag. Looking at her wristband, Lula pumped a fist in the air.

Vert closed the door behind her.

"Made it. I got here before seven!"

The entire study group applauded.

"Whew," she said. "That was close. Vert, are you ready?"

"I am," he said.

Even though he wasn't.

Vert went to stand in the middle of the room.

"Good evening everyone."

He noticed Siffha filming the presentation. This was either the beginning of something wonderful or the end of his career.

"My verse is: *On the twelfth day of Christmas my true love gave to me twelve drummers drumming.* As someone has said before, the last four verses have been mixed up throughout the many versions. Nearly every version then begins to count down all the other days. After each and every verse. If one added up the total number of partridges, turtle doves, etc. in the entire song if it was sung correctly, the number of gifts comes to 364. There are 365 days in an Earth calendar year. A gift for every day but one. The cost must have been enormous."

Vert heard the entrance door woosh open and noise came

from the hallway. He hoped it was Millie and that she'd find where to go.

"But back to drummers. The drums used were similar to the snare drums of today. They were worn off to one side of a human's body, hung by a strap around the neck and over the opposite shoulder. The sound came from beating the drum with two sticks. This verse doesn't seem to contain any symbolism. At the time drummers were used in the military. To communicate with the enemy or to rally the troops. They played in parades and festivals. Orchestras had only just begun to use them, as did the theatre."

A loud anguished sound came from the hallway. Everyone in the study group looked alarmed

"If you'll excuse me for a moment, I will go get my guests. My gifts to this study group, as it were."

Vert bowed and put his hand on the door until it slid open. Then closed it behind him.

He walked down the hallway. The smell was terrible. He'd be paying the community center's cleaning fees.

Millie had arrived and was in place with the largest animal Vert had ever seen. Burt was crooning in the beast's face.

"Good, you found your place. Okay everyone, I'm going to be bringing you in one group at a time. Everyone looks to be in the right order. You can leave your extra belongings here in the hallway if you wish. I think it's going to be quite crowded inside the classroom. No one else will be using the building tonight and there is security on site."

Vert walked to the head of the line.

"Oliver, your group is up first. Follow me."

Vert led the way, opening the door. Then closing it behind the twelve drummers.

Vert said, "I'd like to introduce the Twelve drummers drumming. The Rainy Side Drum Corps." Then he went to stand at the side of the room.

The twelve drummers wore black pants and shirts with green vests. Seven of them wore their drums to the side, like he'd described. Five had larger drums hung from the center of their chests. The larger drums sounded deeper. The smaller drums were pounded on in a faster rhythm. Together the sound was deafening.

Vert smiled inwardly. They were very impressive. The drummers marched in tight patterns around the center of the room. They played two songs. One a bit slower, the other blisteringly fast.

After they finished, the study group applauded. Vert directed the drummers to move to the side of the room. Then he went back out into the hall and got the next group.

He led them into the room. The study group was chatting with the drummers. Everyone looked happy. Good.

"Next we have eleven pipers piping. A different style of pipes from a different region of Europe. Demetri's Pipe Band."

The eleven men and women had dressed in brightly colored flowing blouses, pants and long skirts held up their pan pipes and played. The sounds trilled through the air, soothing his jittered nerves. It seemed like no time at all before they were finished with their two songs. The audience applauded and the band bowed.

Vert directed them to become part of the audience and returned to the hallway, signaling to the next group. The ten males followed him into the classroom.

"I present ten lords a leaping. The Salish Sea Morris Men."

Vert moved back to the doorway and watched as the ten men, dressed all in white, went through their routine. Weaving back and forth and clacking their sticks together in such a complicated manner. He wouldn't even attempt such a thing. The study group was enchanted. Even Pyranz was smiling.

At the end, the study group applauded and the Morris Men searched for places in the room to stand or sit. The classroom was becoming crowded. And stuffy.

Vert went back out into the hallway and motioned to the dancers.

They came up behind him. The one with the bandage on her finger didn't look happy. They all wore what humans called cowboy boots, short skirts and tops which barely covered their mammaries. The costumes were slightly varied, their hair different lengths and colors.

Inside the classroom, Vert said, "The next verse is nine ladies dancing. I chose a different style of dancing than Squip, just for variety. Take it away ladies."

One of them turned on their music. Vert heard the twang of a steel guitar, drums, a bass guitar and a woeful male voice singing, "You've taken your love away, now my life's over."

The females stood in a line and danced to the main rhythm of the music. Turning and kicking and occasionally trading places.

The study group applauded at the end, appreciating the skill. At least Vert assumed the dancing took skill, he wouldn't attempt it.

He moved quickly to the hall. Millie was up next, with her beast. Millie wore a t-shirt and jeans. Her right arm was wrapped and immobilized by a strap around her neck. The beast wore a cloth bag beneath its tail, as if to catch excrement. Vert guessed from the smell of the hallway that the bag was full.

He gestured to her and she led the black and white creature behind her. Millie's friend, a short woman dressed in jeans and a flannel shirt followed.

Millie was a large woman in width and height. Three steps and she'd caught up to Vert.

The beast made him nervous. It looked like an herbivore. A hungry herbivore.

Inside the classroom, Vert said, "I couldn't bring eight maids a-milking. Not in here. So, I brought Millie and, …"

"Jezebel," said Millie. She led the beast into the middle of the room. Her friend carried a short stool and a metal bucket.

Her friend held the beast's rope and Millie's good arm, while she lowered herself onto the stool.

"I tripped the other day and hurt myself. Usually, this is easier. Now Jezebel's a Holstein cow. This breed produces more milk than most others. Jez is a great producer. She's usually milked by a machine, but I use her for school visits, so she's used to this."

Millie began milking the cow with her good hand. Her injured arm still immobilized.

Soon, the only sound that could be heard was the splat, splat, splat of milk being shot into the bucket.

Vert looked at the beast's face. It looked relaxed, relieved even.

When Millie had finished, which seemed to take forever, the audience applauded. Vert realized that even many of the humans had never seen a live cow. He felt sure none of the off-worlders had.

Vert left Millie and her friend to clear the middle of the room and went to get Burt.

Burt and the male who brought the geese, lifted the covered swan box up and then Burt wrapped his huge long arms around it.

"Got it," he said, to the goose male. "Man, I gotta get wheels like yours."

Burt followed Vert down the hallway. Vert opened the double doors this time and Burt went inside. Then Vert closed the doors behind them.

"And here are seven swans, not swimming," said Vert.

Burt whipped the cloth off of the cage. Inside stood seven swans. Stunningly white. They flapped their wings in the cage and gave a strange hoarse honking sound.

"These are mute swans," said Burt. "As you can hear, they ain't mute. Cute little buggers. They originally came from somewhere over where Europe and Asia are joined. People imported them and they like it here."

The swans honked some more. The audience oohed and ahed.

Vert decided that the smell of bird and cow excrement in the room was becoming overpowering. When he went back out into the hallway, he left the double doors open.

He got the burly bearded man with the rolling cage and when Vert returned, Burt and one of the drummers were pulling the cage of swans out of the center.

"I present six geese not a-laying," said Vert, pointing to the rolling cage.

The geese were white and gray. Their bodies looked as large as the swans, but the necks were shorter. And they were clearly incensed about their lot in life. All six of them were hissing at Magwab. Apparently they knew a predator when they saw one.

Magwab laughed. Goose male laughed.

Vert went back into the hallway. He was eager to be finished. He motioned to the next group.

A plump woman wheeled in a covered cage.

"I chose a different interpretation for five. I wasn't as brave as Kleep."

The study group laughed quietly. Kleep's three bodies bowed.

"There's a version of the song that has five hares running. There aren't many hares in this country and humans don't domesticate hares. They're strictly wild creatures. But rabbits are very closely related. So we have five rabbits, not running."

The woman pulled the yellow and white flowered cloth off of the cage. Inside sat five rabbits. One was pure white. A second had white and black fur. Another tan and white. The fourth black and the fifth all brown. The rabbits looked calmly around.

"I show my rabbits," said the woman. "They're used to crowds of people staring at them."

The audience was charmed. The woman nodded at him and pulled her cage off to the side of the room.

Vert returned to the hallway and brought in the next group.

This male carried a black wire cage by the top into the classroom. Inside were four birds.

"Here are four blackbirds," said Vert.

"I'm Jack McNaught. I work for Salish Avian Rescue. These are red-winged blackbirds. Their parents abandoned the nest for some reason and they were found as chicks and brought to us. They're still babies, because they fell behind nutritionally. Next spring, we'll release them and hope they can survive in the wild."

The audience applauded.

Vert would have run to the hallway if he could have. He wanted to get this over with. He felt weak and in need of nutrients, but there was no time for that. He'd used up a lot of energy worrying needlessly.

He signaled the next group. A male carrying a cage. This one wasn't covered.

Inside the classroom, Vert said, "I bring you three French Hens. Or foreign hens. Or three hens."

The tall male said, "I raise Wyandotte chickens. They lay brown eggs. They're easily recognized by the black outline on each of their silver feathers. They lay excellent eggs," said the male.

Vert retreated to the hallway, wishing for a shower. Even a mist bottle. He felt dehydrated.

He said to the female holding a small bird cage, "You're next.

Vert staggered inside to the classroom. "And here are two doves, not turtle doves though."

The female held the cage up. The two pale birds cooed delicately. Then let out a burst of feces. To add to the smell of excrement in the room.

Vert returned to get the last human. The male pulled a cart into the classroom. On the cart stood a potted pear tree. It even had a few unripe pears on it. From one branch hung a metal cage in which sat a partridge.

"A partridge in a pear tree," said Vert. He walked to the doorway and leaned against the frame.

"I'm a keeper from the New Seattle Zoo. This is a gray partridge. She's not from around here, but from Alberta in Canada. They're protected, but someone smuggled her into the states, trying to set up a breeding facility for a private game farm. She was injured and her wing has never healed.

She can't be released back into the wild, so has become a permanent resident at the Zoo. We're in the process of creating her habitat and bringing in five more partridges born in captivity to set up a breeding facility. The pear tree's mine and lives in my garden." He grinned.

The audience clapped.

Vert felt limp.

At that moment, the door to the goose cage opened. Somehow.

Geese poured out, hissing and honking.

Vert moved quickly, closing the doors. Hoping it would make them easier to catch. He longed to be on the other side of the door, but knew it would be a mistake. Just one, piled on top of many.

The goose male was trying to get them back into the cage.

Millie's friend grabbed one of them, but the nasty bird bit her nose. The friend held on and shoved the goose back into the cage, closing the door.

Several of the drummers and Morris Men also tried to catch them.

In the mixup, the cow kicked at a goose, missed and hit the swan cage instead. The door of the swan cage popped open. But only two got out.

Vert climbed up onto a chair as one of the geese cornered him, hissing sinisterly. Goose man grabbed a passing swan.

"I told you this would be fun."

The room was a flurry of flashing humans and white and gray feathers. Many humans and off-worlders shrieked and climbed on top of chairs like Vert.

Others chased after birds and colliding with each other. It was complete chaos.

Magwab caught two birds, one in each paw. The Sartalan looked like he wanted to eat them. Instead he handed one to goose male and the other to Burt.

Worse, Siffha stood on top of the only table.

Filming everything.

Vert wilted.

It took twenty minutes before all the birds were back inside their cages. Everyone laughed hysterically and made jokes.

It didn't help.

Vert felt terrible. This was all his fault. No one else had disasters like this.

Well, the police had come for Kleep's presentation. But no one got hurt.

Lula went to the center of the room. She looked even more disheveled than normal.

"Well, I have to say, this was a most enlightening presentation. Our humble study group can't thank all of you guests enough for coming and participating. I've learned so much during these last few weeks. I didn't know half of the things you all have presented. And Vert has done an astonishing job on his presentation. I can't even imagine what he went through trying to coordinate all of this. Let's give him a big hand."

Everyone clapped. For him. Even the dancer with the bitten finger. And Millie's friend with the bloody nose.

People liked it, despite the disaster.

Vert revived somewhat and bowed.

"Thank you. But my thanks go to all these kind humans who took time out of their busy lives to show up here and help with my humble presentation."

He held out two fronds and flopped them together to indicate clapping as humans did.

The study group clapped. The participants clapped for each other. The geese and swans honked and the beast let out a loud bellow.

Inwardly he glowed. His presentation was a success.

It took a long time for everyone to pack up their birds, animals and belongings, then leave. Siffha was getting ready to leave with them.

"Vert, that was wonderful. Come see me when you get in tomorrow morning. The Embassy has agreed that since you're representing Camassa here, you shouldn't shoulder the entire financial burden. I'm hoping we can completely reimburse you. Gather your records together and let's see what we can do."

Then she was gone.

Vert was so shocked he stood looking at the empty space where she'd been for a full five minutes.

"Vert, are you all right?" asked Lula.

"Yes. I am."

"Good, will you join us?"

Vert looked at the room and found that the study group had formed a small circle of chairs. He took the empty one next to Martha, who sat on the floor.

"Well, again, that was wonderful—all of you. I've loved having you in this study group. I learned so much about Earth and about each of you and your own worlds. I know that everyone's got busy lives. In January, I'll be starting up another study group. If you don't have time, I fully understand. But if you can come, I'd love to see each and every one of you again. Although I think we might need another new rule. No bringing in animals or birds."

The group laughed. Vert smiled.

"What will we be studying next time?" asked Magwab.

Lula wagged a finger back and forth.

"I'm not telling until January. Because some of you will use the next month to get a head start. And I want you to spend the next month observing humans. See what they do at this time of year. Study how they act and what rituals you discover. Join into the ones where you feel comfortable. Many of them are public. There's even a public sing-along of Christmas Carols on Embassy Hill. They always sing *The Twelve Days of Christmas*. A song all of you know intimately now. Then in January, come to the group and ask questions about what you observed."

Magwab seemed to be satisfied with that. Vert was. He just wanted to relax for a few weeks.

Lula passed out a package to everyone. Kleep was only given one, as he was one being, and the Meazza each had their own.

She said, "Don't open these until Christmas Day, December 25. And Merry Christmas. I hope to see you in the New Year."

Then she left, but not before Vert saw tears in her eyes. He knew it was a human expression of sadness or joy. Which had she felt?

Slowly everyone else left, taking their time saying good-byes and seeking reassurance that everyone would come back in January. Vert certainly would.

Vert was the last to leave. It seemed like he should, since he'd hosted tonight. The room was a mess. The chairs had been put upright, but there were feathers and feces everywhere. The bucket of milk had been spilt, leaving a dark spot.

The hallway didn't look a lot better. How many feathers could birds lose and still stay warm?

The cleaning fee would empty his account. It would be good if the Embassy reimbursed him. Otherwise he might not be able to pay for heat.

Vert sighed with relief. It was done. It had been a success.

He switched off the lights. Then closed the doors and took his plasticoat off the hook where it had hung since he'd arrived. He slipped on the shoes.

Vert walked out into the cold night air and down the sidewalk to his condo. The clouds had cleared and the moonless sky shone bright with stars. His birth world was out there, not visible from Earth.

Camassa no longer felt like home. This strange planet with even stranger animals was home now.

Home.

He opened the door and walked in, took off his plasticoat, kicked off the shoes and went to stand in the nutrient bath. Everything here was warm. And life was perfect.

If you have five minutes, would you kindly go to the online store where you normally buy books, or Amazon, or Goodreads and leave a review? It doesn't need to be long, just a few words about your reactions to the stories or characters while they're still fresh in your mind.

Reviews helps other readers feel confident taking a chance on finding a book they might enjoy. Your help is very much appreciated.

Thank you!

ABOUT THE AUTHOR

Linda Jordan writes fascinating characters, visionary worlds, and imaginative fiction. She creates both long and short fiction, serious and silly. She believes in the power of healing and transformation, and many of her stories follow those themes.

In a previous lifetime, Linda coordinated the Clarion West Writers' Workshop as well as the Reading Series. She spent four years as Chair of the Board of Directors during Clarion West's formative period. She's also worked as a travel agent, a baker, and a pond plant/fish sales person, you know, the sort of things one does as a writer.

Currently, she's the Programming Director for the Writers Cooperative of the Pacific Northwest.

Linda now lives in the rainy wilds of Washington state with her husband, daughter, four cats, a cluster of Koi and an infinite number of slugs and snails.

Her other work includes:
Titanian Fury
Falling Into Flight
Love & the Aliens
Aboard the Universe
To the Stars & Back Again
All her work can be found at your favorite online bookseller.

Get a FREE ebook!

Sign up for Linda's Serendipitous Newsletter at her website:
www.LindaJordan.net

She can be found on Facebook at:
www.facebook.com/LindaJordanWriter

Metamorphosis Press website is at:
www.MetamorphosisPress.com

Goodreads: https://www.goodreads.com/author/show/
2021274.Linda_Jordan

Writers love reviews, even short, simple ones. Honest reviews help other readers find the book. Please go to where you bought this book, or Goodreads, and leave a review. It would be much appreciated.

www.ingramcontent.com/pod-product-compliance
Lightning Source LLC
Chambersburg PA
CBHW021329190726
48288CB00003B/1015